Books

M000191694

Historical Western Romance Series

MacLarens of Fire Mountain

Tougher than the Rest, Book One
Faster than the Rest, Book Two
Harder than the Rest, Book Three
Stronger than the Rest, Book Four
Deadlier than the Rest, Book Five
Wilder than the Rest, Book Six

Redemption Mountain

Redemption's Edge, Book One
Wildfire Creek, Book Two
Sunrise Ridge, Book Three
Dixie Moon, Book Four
Survivor Pass, Book Five
Promise Trail, Book Six
Deep River, Book Seven
Courage Canyon, Book Eight
Forsaken Falls, Book Nine
Solitude Gorge, Book Ten, Coming next in the
series!

MacLarens of Boundary Mountain

Colin's Quest, Book One,
Brodie's Gamble, Book Two

Quinn's Honor, Book Three
Sam's Legacy, Book Four
Heather's Choice, Book Five
Nate's Destiny, Book Six, Coming next in the series!

Contemporary Romance Series

MacLarens of Fire Mountain

Second Summer, Book One
Hard Landing, Book Two
One More Day, Book Three
All Your Nights, Book Four
Always Love You, Book Five
Hearts Don't Lie, Book Six
No Getting Over You, Book Seven
'Til the Sun Comes Up, Book Eight
Foolish Heart, Book Nine
Forever Love, Book Ten, Coming next in the series!

Peregrine Bay

Reclaiming Love, Book One, A Novella
Our Kind of Love, Book Two

Burnt River

Shane's Burden, Book One by Peggy Henderson
Thorn's Journey, Book Two by Shirleen Davies
Aqua's Achilles, Book Three by Kate Cambridge

Ashley's Hope, Book Four by Amelia Adams
Harpur's Secret, Book Five by Kay P. Dawson
Mason's Rescue, Book Six by Peggy L. Henderson
Del's Choice, Book Seven by Shirleen Davies
Ivy's Search, Book Eight by Kate Cambridge
Phoebe's Fate, Book Nine by Amelia Adams
Brody's Shelter, Book Ten by Kay P. Dawson
Boone's Surrender, Book Eleven by Shirleen Davies
Watch for more books in the series!

The best way to stay in touch is to subscribe to my newsletter. Go to www.shirleendavies.com and subscribe in the box at the top of the right column that asks for your email. You'll be notified of new books before they are released, have chances to win great prizes, and receive other subscriber-only specials.

Nate's Destiny

**MacLarens of Boundary Mountain
Historical Western Romance Series**

SHIRLEEN DAVIES

**Book Six in the MacLarens of
Boundary Mountain**

Historical Western Romance Series

For permission requests, contact the publisher.

Avalanche Ranch Press, LLC
PO Box 12618
Prescott, AZ 86304

Nate's Destiny is a work of fiction. Names, characters, places, and incidents are either products of the author's imagination or used fictitiously. Any resemblance to actual events, locales, or persons, living or dead, is wholly coincidental.

Book design and conversions by Joseph Murray at 3rdplanetpublishing.com

Cover design by Kim Killion, The Killion Group

ISBN: 978-1-941786-62-8

I care about quality, so if you find something in error, please contact me via email at
shirleen@shirleendavies.com

Description

Nate's Destiny, Book Six, MacLarens of Boundary Mountain Historical Western Romance Series

Nate Hollis had everything, until a Confederate cannonball changed the course of his life. His job as a deputy in Conviction and his love for a beautiful woman allows him to dream of a future he once thought lost. He never counted on the gnawing pain of his injury and the craving for relief to spiral him downward into a man he hardly recognizes.

Geneen MacGregor feels blessed to be considered a part of the MacLaren family and a valued member of their ranch. Her love for Nate provides the dream of someday marrying and having a family of her own—until she wakes one morning to find him gone.

To escape his persistent hunger for opium, Nate travels a few hours north to a small town along the Feather River. A job at the livery allows him to envision a new start where he's free from the insidious drug and once again able to be the man Geneen deserves.

The invitation to join her good friends at their ranch near Settlers Valley is what she needs to rid Nate from her mind. After months without word, Geneen is certain the man she loves with all her heart has forgotten her.

Then an accidental encounter brings more anger than forgiveness, more questions than answers. A second chance seems as far away as ever with neither able to bridge the gap between them.

Their efforts to mend the past stall as a series of dangerous events forces Nate to help an old friend, and a monster from the past poses a new threat to the people of Settlers Valley.

Can two people, once so much in love, heal the wounds of the past to create a future brighter than either had ever imagined?

Nate's Destiny, book six in the MacLarens of Boundary Mountain Historical Western Romance Series, is a stand-alone, full-length novel with an HEA and no cliffhanger.

Visit my website for a list of characters for each series.

http://www.shirleendavies.com/character-list.html

Dedication

Nate's Destiny is dedicated to my dear friend who passed away early in 2018. We met in junior high and remained life-long friends. Barb, you will always be the sister of my heart.

Acknowledgements

As always, many thanks to my husband for reading every chapter as soon as it's written, my editor, Kim Young, proofreader, Alicia Carmical, Joseph Murray, who is superb at formatting my books for print and electronic versions, and my cover designer, Kim Killion.

Nate's Destiny

Prologue

Battle of Brandy Station, Virginia
June 9, 1863

Union Cavalry Captain Nathan Hollis focused his field glasses northeast. The pre-dawn light made it virtually impossible to spot the Rappahannock River from this distance. His orders were clear. Wait for Union Major General Alfred Pleasonton to give the signal before engaging Confederate General J.E.B. Stuart's seasoned cavalry.

Nate nearly salivated at the chance to engage the famed Confederate horse soldier. Ever since the 16th Pennsylvania Cavalry had been organized September 1862 in his hometown of Harrisburg, he and his men wanted nothing more than to face the legendary Southern brigade. They'd already fought numerous battles, honing their skills, doing all they could to gain the respect of the leaders of the Union Army of the Potomac. The time had come to put all their hard work to the test.

Lowering the glasses, Nate glanced at his regiment spread out on either side of him. Keeping their horses in check, weapons at the ready, they waited for his order. His own stallion, a horse bred on the family farm and trained over many months, didn't flinch. Nate couldn't imagine going into battle with any other animal beneath him.

"Captain. Look to the northeast." First Lieutenant George Kellogg, a man Nate trusted with his life, pointed at a flash of light. "I believe Pleasonton has begun his attack."

Reining his horse toward the river, he lifted the glasses once more, spotting another flash of light. "It's time to move out, Kellogg."

Sliding the glasses into a sheath, Captain Hollis lifted his arm, glanced around at the eager faces, then lowered it in one strong, decisive move. A rush of excitement overtook him as he watched over two thousand men astride their war-trained horses thunder across the valley.

Racing toward the target, the men could no longer contain their silence. Sabers drawn, they controlled their horses with one hand, bending over the saddle horn as they rushed forward. Gunbelts holding a Colt revolver were strapped around their waists. Nate and a few of his men were fortunate enough to have rifles secured in scabbards. He'd drawn the weapon in only one battle, preferring the saber in close combat.

The orders had been to dismount at an engagement and continue the fight on foot. It didn't take long for Nate to realize this tactic wouldn't work in the chaos resulting from their surprise attack against the experienced Confederate cavalry led by Stuart.

Signaling his men to stay mounted, he led the attack, heading into the thick mass of Southern fighters. Swinging his saber, Nate cut down one man, then another, reining his horse around to face two more mounted defenders. With each strike, he felt both the exhilaration of battle and the regret at ending a life. He couldn't dwell on the latter. Nate and his regiment had a job to do. If successful, it could bring an end to the war and usher in the peace he greatly desired.

Hearing the clanking of sabers and the distant thunder of cannons, he glanced up toward St. James Church and the river beyond. For a moment, he paused, mesmerized by the sight of the 6th Pennsylvania Cavalry charging the Confederate guns positioned at the church. He would later learn the regiment, led by a friend and mentor, suffered the greatest causalities in the battle.

Shouts turned Nate's attention to a group of three Confederates charging toward him. Dropping his reins, he held the saber in his left hand, drawing the Colt with his right. In quick succession, he cut down the riders, leaving their horses to run aimlessly among the battle.

Continuing his assault, concentrating on the Confederate cavalry storming toward him, Nate failed to see Southern cannoneers on the nearby hill swing their guns in his direction. A burst of light, followed by a panicked scream, warned him of the danger.

Shifting in the saddle, he slid the Colt into the holster, lifting his saber. Too late, Nate saw another flash of light, a dark ball slicing through the air toward him. Pain like he'd never felt tore through him at the same time his stallion reared back, hurling him to the ground. Landing on his back, Nate tried to push up, excruciating pain in his left arm causing him to fall back down.

His head spun and body throbbed as he fought to stay conscious. Knowing this fight was impossible, he turned his head, glancing to the side. Next to him lay his prized stallion, a rapidly darkening hole in his side, the horse's panicked eyes looking to Nate for comfort his master couldn't give.

Ignoring his own pain, he shifted enough to draw the Colt from its holster. Tears stinging his eyes, Nate murmured a few soft words, then a tender goodbye before pulling the trigger. He felt a searing ache in his chest as the gun dropped from his hand.

Glancing to his injured left side, he tried to lift his arm. A silent scream tore through his head a moment before sweet oblivion claimed him.

Chapter One

Nate's body shook so hard, his teeth rattled. He knew the tremors were a combination of the cold night and his body's continued insistence it required the opium he'd refused to provide. The fact no stove existed in the cramped shack his employer allowed him to use didn't help. He'd huddled by a fire outside as long as possible before giving up, taking refuge in the tiny structure that had become his home. If his horse would've fit, Nate would've brought Nomad inside the shack for warmth.

He used his right hand to drape the last blanket over him, tucking it around what was left of his left arm. Leaning back against the rough wood walls, he stared out the lone window. The winter sky darkened early these days, the temperature dropping into the early thirties by seven in the evening.

Nate had experienced worse while fighting for the 16th Pennsylvania Cavalry. The regiment, part of the Army of the Potomac, had spent many nights in bleak conditions, surrounded by snow drifts over three feet high.

Rubbing his right hand along his thighs for warmth, Nate mumbled a raspy thanks to his employer for providing the derelict shack as part of Nate's wages. Without it, he'd be hunched over a fire on the outskirts of town.

He'd stumbled onto the job not long after arriving in Settlers Valley, a month after his gutless departure from Circle M, the MacLaren's ranch a day's ride south of the small town. Marcus Kamm had shaken his head when Nate inquired about the job posted on the door of the livery.

The left arm he'd lost below the elbow during the Battle of Brandy Station caused many to turn him away. This time, Nate fought for a chance to prove he could do what Marcus needed. After two days, the livery owner relented. Marcus got a hardworking laborer, and Nate received what he and Nomad needed to survive.

Almost two months had passed since he walked through the livery door, and every day Nate said a prayer, thanking Marcus for giving him a chance. Burrowing deeper into the blanket, he continued to stare out the window, thinking of how his life had changed so much in a few short years.

At twenty-one, he'd been engaged to a beautiful woman with a gracious smile and genteel manner. They'd grown up together in Harrisburg, Pennsylvania, promising themselves to each other by their seventeenth birthdays. By the time he'd turned twenty-three, his captain's rank had placed him in a prominent position within the 16th Pennsylvania Cavalry. A few months later, they'd sent him home. His regiment had distinguished themselves at Brandy Station, but in the process, Nate had lost much of his left arm, his prized stallion, and his sense of purpose. A week later, his fiancée broke their engagement, unable to cope with his change in status.

When Nate's father gifted him Nomad, a four-year-old bay gelding, he'd saddled his new horse and informed his parents he intended to head west. His mother's arguments to stay didn't sway him, nor did the tears she swiped from her cheeks the morning of his departure. His father, a veteran of the Mexican-American War, clasped him on the back, pulling him into a hug.

When you find yourself, Nathan, come home. There'll always be a place for you here, his father had told him, his voice cracking as his son mounted Nomad and rode away.

A year and a half had passed since that day, and Nate felt no closer to finding himself than he had the day he rode off, leaving his mother, father, and siblings behind.

"Thought you could use these."

Nate glanced up, startled to see Marcus standing in the doorway, two more blankets clutched in his hands.

"Esther insisted you'd need more than the ones you have." Stepping inside, Marcus set the blankets on the cot, raising his hand when Nate moved to get up. "Stay where you are. I'm headed back to the house."

Nodding, Nate picked up one of the blankets. "Thank your sister for me."

"I don't know why, but she's got a soft spot for you, Hollis." Marcus opened his mouth to say more when Nate shook his head, a slow grin tipping up the corners of his mouth.

"You don't have to say it, Marcus. I already know to keep my thoughts off Esther."

Crossing his arms, the broad-shouldered, half-German, half-Jewish livery owner leaned against the doorframe. "Nothing against you. You're a fine man and a hard worker. But anyone can see you've got demons chasing you."

They'd never discussed Nate's dependence on opium or how he'd come to Settlers Valley, hoping to rid it from his body. Somehow, the heinous drug hadn't made its way into the small town where he'd found refuge.

"No need to explain, Marcus. Truth is, I'm no good for any woman, least of all Esther."

Marcus didn't deny it as he dropped his arms to his sides. "She wants you to join us for supper tomorrow night, and I don't want to hear any arguments, Hollis."

Nate smirked. "You won't hear any complaints from me. Tell her it would be my pleasure to eat her home cooking instead of beans and hardtack."

Snorting, Marcus started to turn away, then stopped. "I've got a wood stove coming on the next stage. I expect you to figure a way to use it."

Nate didn't know why, but the kind gesture struck his heart, a lump forming in his throat. "Thank you, Marcus," he mumbled, glancing away.

"Don't thank me. It's another of Esther's ideas."

"I'll thank her when I come to supper tomorrow night."

"Be sure you do." Marcus closed the door behind him, stopping the wind from chilling the shack even more.

Grabbing the extra blankets, Nate spread them over his still shaking body. Within minutes, he began to relax, his muscles slackening as his body warmed. This was when he allowed himself to think of Geneen MacGregor, Sarah MacLaren's sister, the woman he'd left behind at Circle M.

Two weeks before, he'd spotted Quinn, Blaine, and Heather MacLaren, along with Caleb Stewart having breakfast at the only restaurant in Settlers Valley. Keeping well out of sight, he'd watched them leave, riding north along the Feather River.

Marcus solved the mystery of their arrival when he mentioned elderly rancher Archie Galloway selling his spread to a young cowboy who'd worked for Circle M.

A few days later, he'd been stunned to see Geneen and a few more MacLarens ride into town. Nate had watched in silence as they gathered in the church to watch Caleb and Heather wed. He'd hidden in the shadows, unable to keep his gaze off Geneen. Now he spent a good deal of his time figuring out a way to continue working for Marcus without her, Heather, or Caleb discovering him.

He'd thought of moving on, not taking the chance of being seen before he rid his body of the drug he continued to crave. Two things stopped him. Few men were eager to hire someone with an almost useless arm, and most towns of any size included a population of Chinese, the suppliers of the opium he forced himself to avoid.

He woke each day, his mind still craving the vile substance, even if his body had begun to grow accustomed to living without it. Several strong cups of coffee laced with a small amount of whiskey helped tame the hunger still circling in his head.

Doc Vickery in Conviction, the town closest to Circle M, had warned him he might never completely lose the mental craving for the drug. Nate had scoffed at the assertion, believing if his body didn't need it, neither would his head. He'd been wrong.

Until the day came when opium no longer held any power over him, he'd stay as far away from Geneen as possible. And if she discovered him living in Settlers Valley, Nate would do and say whatever he had to in order to keep her away from him and his demons.

Highlander Ranch

Geneen leaned the shovel against a stall, breathing a deep sigh of relief. She'd been mucking out the barn for the last two days, undeterred by the amount of work.

At eighty, Archie no longer had the strength to handle the everyday chores of running a ranch. He'd focused his time and energy on keeping the animals fed and the cows milked. Mending fences, cleaning stalls, and basic repairs had gone unattended for what appeared to be years.

More than two weeks had passed since the wedding, and between Caleb, Heather, and Geneen, they'd accomplished a great deal. So much, the young couple hoped she wouldn't return to Circle M in the near future.

After Nate left Circle M, she'd felt adrift, unable to focus on a future without him. For the first time in months, she felt needed.

"How are you doing in here?"

Spinning around, Geneen smiled at Heather. "Just finished. I'll head into the house in a bit to start supper."

Removing the saddle and bridle from Shamrock, Heather let the mare into the pasture behind the barn. Returning to stand next to Geneen, she crossed her arms, leaning a shoulder against a stall.

"Caleb received a telegram from Uncle Ewan. He wants to know if we'll be riding back to Circle M for Christmas. Archie said he'd be doing fine here alone."

Lifting a brow, Geneen brushed her hands down the pants she wore around the ranch. "What do *you* want to do?"

Heather shrugged. "I miss the family, but I'll be doing whatever Caleb thinks best. This is a bigger ranch than I thought and there's a lot needing to be done. What would you be thinking?"

Pacing a few feet away, she looked out the barn door to the hills in the distance. "The first Christmas in your new home is important. I know Sarah will understand if I stay here with you."

Chuckling, Heather pushed away from the stall. "Aye. Your sister is the most understanding lass I know. You being happy is what means the most to her."

Geneen turned toward her, a relaxed smile on her face. "Then we'll be here for Christmas. We can travel to Circle M in the spring."

"Aye. That's what Caleb is thinking. We'll be moving part of the herd south to join with their cattle when they make the drive to Sacramento. He thinks the three of us can move what we have without trouble."

Nodding, Geneen shoved a strand of hair from her face. "It depends on how many head Caleb decides to take. I heard at the general store there are some men looking for work."

"Mr. Kamm at the livery told Caleb the man working for him has some experience. He might be interested in extra work."

Geneen's brows knit together. "I didn't know he had someone else working for him."

Heather shrugged. "Caleb didn't, either. The lad must be working in back. Mr. Kamm also said there'll be a dance in town this Saturday. I'm thinking we should all go. It would be good to meet more of our neighbors."

Letting out a slow breath, Geneen grabbed the shovel, carrying it to the tool closet in the barn. "Why don't you and Caleb go? I'd be happy to stay here and keep watch on the ranch."

Heather shook her head and laughed. "Nae, lass. You love to dance. We'll not be leaving you behind."

Groaning, Geneen shoved her hands into her coat pockets as she walked out of the barn toward the house, hearing Heather hurry to catch up to her.

"I know what you're thinking, and I'm not interested."

A slight grin tipped up the corners of Heather's mouth. "And what would I be thinking?"

"You and Caleb want me to meet someone, forget about Nate."

"It would be good for you, lass. You've not heard from him in months. Nobody has. He could've left the state and ridden back east, maybe back home to Pennsylvania."

Geneen bit her lower lip, her chin rising in defiance. "Jinny didn't know if Sam would return, either, but she waited for him." The mention of Heather's cousin and what she went through waiting for the man she loved to return to Conviction caused them both to sober.

"'Tis true. But Sam knew where to find Jinny. Nate would be having no idea you're with me and Caleb in Settlers Valley. Besides, I'm not thinking of more than you having some fun. For all we know, there'll not be any handsome, single men at the dance."

Geneen snorted. They both knew that was a lie. She and Heather had already met a few single ranch hands during their visits to town, and she had no doubt several would be at the dance. If only she could rid her thoughts of Nate.

Geneen had been drawn to him from the first day they'd met, not long after he'd taken a job as one of Brodie's deputies. Her gaze had taken in the determined set of his jaw, eyes that missed nothing, and his defensive stance, daring anyone to think less of him because of his missing left arm. He'd compensated well for the loss of the limb.

Already an accomplished rider, his skills handling a horse increased, as did his expertise with a six-shooter and rifle. He'd taken a job as a lawman in Abilene before continuing his journey west. That experience, plus the fact he'd fought off three men when he first arrived in Conviction, made a huge impact on Brodie, influencing his decision to hire Nate.

16

She and Nate had become close, sitting next to each other at Sunday suppers and church. He hadn't hesitated to ask her to dance at the community shindigs, monopolizing her time, becoming surly when other men asked to cut in. Those had been good times, until the pain in his left arm drove him to the opium dens in Conviction.

Bringing him to Circle M helped rid his body of the need for the insidious substance. But no matter what she and the MacLaren family did, nothing rid Nate's mind of the crushing need for opium. One morning, he'd packed what little he had, saddled Nomad, and rode off, telling no one of his destination or possible return.

That was the last anyone saw or heard from him.

"You're right. I'd like to attend the dance, even if the only single men are as old as my father." Shrugging out of her heavy coat, Geneen hung it up before entering the kitchen to pull out what she needed for supper.

Heather moved next to her, placing a hand on her arm, then smiled. "That's the spirit, lass. You have a few days to figure out what we'll be wearing."

"Me?" Geneen squeaked. "Jinny is the one good at dressing us, not me."

"Well, she's not here," Heather chuckled. "It's not as if we have much to choose from."

Cutting the meat, Geneen glanced over her shoulder. "We'll both decide. If needed, we'll go to town and buy ribbons for our hair." She paused, thinking of the last time she'd received a new ribbon. It had been from Nate. A present for her birthday. Shaking off the melancholy too often ruling her days, Geneen drew in a slow breath, focusing on the meal she prepared. "Perhaps we'll even find new hats."

"Nae, lass. You're the one to wear them. I look foolish with my hair going in all directions."

Geneen shook her head. "It's easy to remedy, Heather. We'll buy new hats and I'll fix your hair. You'll look so different, Caleb won't even recognize you."

Opening a tin, she pulled out an oatmeal cake and took a bite. "Aye. That's what worries me."

The kitchen door opened. Caleb walked inside, his hands caked in mud. "What worries you, sweetheart?" He walked up to his wife, meaning to put his arms around her.

Holding up her hands, Heather backed away. "Ach. You'll not be touching me with those hands."

Looking at them, as if he hadn't noticed all the dirt, he shrugged, moving to the sink. "What has you worried?"

Brushing cake crumbs from her mouth, Heather wiped her hands down her pants. "We've been talking of going to the dance Saturday night."

"And what to wear," Geneen added.

Drying his hands, Caleb's brows drew together. "You'll wear one of your dresses. What else?"

Glancing at Heather, Geneen burst into laughter. "How clever of you, Caleb."

"What did I say?" He looked at each of them in genuine confusion.

"She's jesting with you, love." Heather picked up an onion and began to peel the skin. "We've not much to choose from and would like to go to town for ribbons and perhaps new hats." Her brows drew into a frown. "If we've the money for them."

All three knew the low funds they lived on each month. It would change after they'd driven the first herd to market in the spring.

Geneen shook her head. "It was a foolish idea, Caleb. Heather and I have all we need to look splendid for the dance."

Bending down, he placed a kiss on Heather's cheek. "We've the money for hats. I've got to see Mr. Kamm about repairing the harness. The breast collar is broken and I don't have what I need to fix it. How about we ride in tomorrow morning? You can get what you need while I meet with Mr. Kamm."

Standing, Heather wrapped her arms around his neck. "That would be grand. We'll be at the general store when it opens."

A soft smile played across Caleb's face as he looked down at her. "That we will." Kissing her quickly, he left the kitchen, drawing in a deep breath.

He'd make certain his wife and Geneen got new hats and whatever ribbon they wanted, even if it meant growing the account at the general store to an unreasonable amount. If he could only afford one ranch hand, they'd be able to make twice the progress. Someone who might agree to a clean, warm place to sleep and meals, waiting for their wages until spring. Scrubbing a hand down his face, Caleb climbed the stairs, his mind reeling from all the work needing to be done.

Chapter Two

Settlers Valley

Nate stilled at the sound of the familiar voice coming from the front of the livery. He'd recognize Caleb Stewart's deep tone and slight brogue anywhere. Unlike most of the MacLarens, few would even recognize his Scottish roots, believing him born in America rather than the Highlands of Scotland. The same was true of Sarah and Geneen. Their brogues were so modest, they were seldom noticed.

"I've got the new ranch sign you ordered. I'll have my hired man bring it out."

Nate's breath hitched at Marcus's offer. He needed to disappear out the back, hoping his boss would assume he'd taken a break to use the facilities. Caleb discovering him in Settlers Valley wouldn't be wise for anyone.

"Save it for my next trip. I didn't bring the wagon." Caleb held up the broken harness.

Marcus took it from his hand, examining the damage. "Ah, I can see why you'd leave it at the ranch. My man can have this repaired in a few hours, if you have the time to wait."

Caleb shook his head. "I've got too much work to do. I'll ride back on Friday. The women

21

want to attend the dance on Saturday night, and it wouldn't do to have them all dressed up and riding their horses." He smiled on the last, seeing an understanding nod from Marcus.

"My sister, Esther, wants to go. I'm not much for dances, but she doesn't get to enjoy herself much anymore." Studying the harness once more, he set it aside. "I'll make certain this is ready for you on Friday."

"Thanks, Mr. Kamm."

"I'm not an old man, Caleb. My name's Marcus."

Caleb grasped the hand held out toward him. "Marcus it is then. I'll see you Friday."

Nate poked his head around the outside corner of the livery, watching as Caleb mounted Jupiter, reining him toward the other end of town. A strange pain sliced through him as his friend rode away. Not for the first time, he cursed his luck at the Battle of Brandy Station.

The Union Army surgeon had encouraged him to be thankful for his luck. If the cannonball had been a few inches to the right, Nate would've died. In his mind, if it had been a few inches to his left, he'd have his left arm and his beloved horse would still be alive. And he wouldn't be fighting the cravings for a remedy that eased the pain but inflicted havoc on his life.

"Nate. Caleb Stewart brought this in to be repaired." Marcus held up the halter. "I told him it could be ready Friday."

Pushing his regrets aside, he took the halter, studying the broken leather. "I can have it fixed by then."

"Good." Turning to leave, Marcus stopped, looking back at Nate. "There's a dance Saturday night. Most everyone in town will be there."

Nate waited, looking up when Marcus didn't continue. "I'm not planning on going."

"You might want to reconsider. There will be some fine-looking women who want nothing more than a night of dancing."

Snorting, Nate held up the stub of his left arm. "I don't do much dancing anymore, Marcus."

"Even I know you don't need a full arm to dance, Hollis. Fact is, you don't have to dance at all. You can do like me and just talk to a few people."

A wry grin turned up the corners of Nate's mouth. "Esther will expect me to ask her to dance."

Crossing his arms, Marcus studied him a moment before his features relaxed. "She'll not embarrass you, if that's what worries you."

"I'd never worry about Esther embarrassing me. My worry is about embarrassing her. It's a chance for her to meet someone good, a man who'll be able to give her a good life. That man isn't me, Marcus."

"Hell, I'm not asking you to marry my sister. We've already had that discussion. All I'm talking about is you joining the rest of us to meet some of the townsfolk. Might do you some good." He looked at the ground, shaking his head, then glanced back up. "I'd best get back up front."

Nate hung his head as Marcus closed the door behind him. No matter what his boss said, he knew he'd never attend the dance. Hearing Caleb say Heather and Geneen would be going didn't provide an incentive. Instead, the knowledge she'd be so close, yet still so far from his grasp only drove the knife deeper into his chest.

The same as Esther, Geneen deserved someone whole, complete, who could provide what he never could. Not until he drove the desire for opium from his mind, which he'd begun to believe would never happen. The days ran together, one bleeding into the next with little to distinguish them.

Nate had few options. Not many men were like Marcus, willing to hire someone with the use of one arm. An expert horseman, crack shot, and capable of defending himself with his right arm only, Nate found himself in the position of constantly having to prove his abilities. Prove his worth to a doubting world. Worse, he had to confirm his worth to himself, make it through each day without going crazy from depriving his mind of the opium it demanded. It was a life he had to face alone.

Shouts from the front of the livery had him dropping the tool he held and hurrying through the door. Standing inches from Marcus was a slender man of average height, his face twisted in anger, a finger of his right hand jabbing his boss in the chest. For an instant, Nate wondered how long it would take for Marcus, much taller and more muscular, to swat the man's hand away before landing a blow to his chin.

"I'll have the work to you when it's ready, Leland, and not an hour before."

The well-dressed man glared at Marcus, inching closer. "I know what we agreed, but I need it now, Kamm. I'm willing to pay you double if I can have it by tonight."

Rubbing his brow, Marcus shook his head. "It isn't possible. You've given me a new design for your dredge, one I've never built before. I'm halfway there and planned to have it finalized by Tuesday."

Leland huffed out a frustrated breath. "That's almost another week." He ground out the words as if they were painful to say.

"Which is what we agreed. Do you want it quick or right, Leland?"

"Both, dammit. If you can't do it, I'll take my business elsewhere."

Marcus's gaze narrowed on the owner of the richest gold mine on the Feather River. "You're welcome to find someone else. You paid me half in advance, which is how far I've gotten. You can take the plans and what I've done. We'll call it even."

Pacing several feet away, Leland settled his hands on his hips, staring out at the bustling street. Turning, he glared at Marcus. "You know there's no one else to do the work within a hundred miles."

"Well now, I don't know that for a fact, but it's fair to say you'd be hard-pressed to find someone with my experience who can finish it by tomorrow night." Marcus leaned a hip against his workbench, crossing his arms. "I've been doing the work alone. If I have my hired hand help, we might be able to have it finished by Sunday night. We've got a couple other orders to finish. We'll do our best, but I can't guarantee anything."

Nate glanced between the two men. One, a hard as nails blacksmith with a quick mind and natural business sense. The other, an East Coast lawyer who seized the ownership of a profitable gold mine when one of his clients died without heirs. For now, neither had noticed him standing at the back, listening to every word spoken.

"Who's this man of yours?" Leland asked. "I want to meet him."

"And you will." Turning to head outside, Marcus stopped at the sight of Nate standing a few feet away. "Ah, here he is now. Nate, this is Leland Nettles, owner of the Acorn Gold Mine up north a ways. Leland, this is Nate Hollis, the best man who's ever worked for me."

Nate stepped forward, extending his hand. "It's a pleasure, Mr. Nettles."

Leland's gaze moved to his left side, his eyes widening. "You've got only part of your left arm."

Dropping his hand, Nate smirked. "It's what happens when a rebel cannonball hits you during battle. I survived. My horse didn't."

Ignoring Nate, he looked at Marcus. "You say this man is the best you have?"

"He's *all* I have, and I'm glad he's here. You heard my terms. Accept them or take your design and find someone else." Turning his back on Nettles, Marcus picked up the tool he'd been forging while Nate spun around to head back to the livery.

"Wait."

Both turned at Leland's resigned voice.

He looked at Nate, not at all apologetic for his rude behavior. "Fine. I'll be here Sunday night, and it had best be ready."

"As I said, Leland, we'll do our best, but can't guarantee it. The design is complex. I don't know what problems we might encounter. The worst case is what we agreed. Tuesday. I want to make sure you understand what I'm saying."

"Dammit, Marcus. I can understand English perfectly well. I just don't like the options."

"Neither do I, but it's all I've got to offer." Marcus held out his hand, waiting until Leland accepted it. "We're in agreement then."

"Send word to me when it's finished." Stomping out of the livery, they could hear his mumbled curses all the way to his horse.

"You say the man owns the Acorn Mine?" Nate stood just inside the livery, watching as Leland reined his horse around, wincing when he angrily kicked the animal hard to get it moving.

"He does. Picked it up cheap when his client died suddenly. Nothing about it ever seemed quite right to me, but the judge who came through said it was all legal. Why?"

"Just doesn't seem too hospitable is all." Nate idly scratched a spot on his left forearm.

Marcus stopped his work to glance over his shoulder. "Never has been. Expects people to jump when he speaks. And most people do."

"Not you, though."

Marcus shook his head. "No. Not me."

Walking past him, Nate stopped at the back door, a sardonic smile on his face. "Guess I'd better get the harness fixed and the other work done. I wouldn't mind getting Nettles his order early. Best to have the man obliged to you rather than the other way around."

Glancing up, Marcus nodded, a slight grin marring his otherwise taciturn expression.

"What do you think of this one, Geneen?" Heather held up a spool of moss green ribbon which matched her eyes.

Walking up to her, Geneen pursed her lips as she compared the green ribbon to the blue ribbon Heather held in her other hand. "Both are pretty. The green one would be better with the hat you selected."

Setting the blue one back on the shelf, Heather scrunched her face. "Maybe I'll just be wearing the ribbon."

"I thought we agreed the hat you selected would be perfect with your dress. We'll use the ribbon on your hair to keep it pulled back."

"Tame it, you mean." Heather had always struggled to keep her light brown hair in place.

"All right. I'll be getting both. And what about you, lass? Did you decide on a hat?"

Geneen fingered her deep red hair as she stared at the hat. It had ribbons of emerald green and bright blue, perfect for the dress she planned to wear. She had no money of her own, and it didn't seem right having Caleb pay for such an extravagance.

"Ach, you're thinking too much, lass." Heather placed a hand on Geneen's arm. "I don't know what Caleb and I'd be doing without you. It's sure not as much work would be getting done. Let us buy the hat and ribbon."

The sound of boots on the wooden floor had them both glancing at the front.

"Tell her, Caleb."

Lifting a brow, he glanced between the two women. "Tell her what, Heather?"

"You'll be buying the hats and ribbons for us both. It's only right with all the work the lass has been doing."

He smiled at Geneen. "I never thought otherwise. Now, if you're both ready, I'll pay so we can start back to the ranch. I've two days' worth of work to finish in eight hours." Taking the hats and ribbon from their hands, he took them to the counter as the ladies continued to study other items. "I'd like these put on my account, along with this, Mr. Beall." He reached into his pocket, pulling out some coins.

Thomas Beall, owner of Beall's General Store, glanced down at the coins. "I'm happy to put it toward what you owe, Caleb, but you're welcome to wait until the end of the month. I know you're good for it."

"If you don't mind, I'd rather do it now. I'm certain the ladies will be doing more shopping before Christmas, and I don't want to be too far in debt to you."

The corners of Beall's eyes crinkled. "As you wish. I know the MacLarens will step in to help if needed." He scooped up the coins, not seeing the flash of red on Caleb's cheeks.

"It's certain they have a good reputation, but I plan to run Highlander Ranch without their help." His words were spoken softly and edged with a hard determination.

"I meant no offense. Word is you're a hard worker, and frugal. Nothing wrong with either of those, or wanting to do it all on your own." He pulled a ledger from under the counter and made a few notes. "I expect you and the women will be coming to the dance."

Caleb turned to see Heather and Geneen smiling over a bottle of bath salts. "The ladies wouldn't miss it."

Thomas threw his head back and laughed. "All the women love dances. Me? I like the food, music, and the time away from the store. If I never had to dance again, I'd be a happy man."

Nodding, Caleb picked up the hats and ribbon. "I'm fortunate. My wife isn't much of a dancer. Spares me the embarrassment. I'd best get the women and head back. There's a lot of work to be done before Saturday."

"I'll see you at the dance, Caleb."

Thomas watched him usher the women outside and mount their horses. He knew good people when he met them, and the Stewarts were a welcome addition to Settlers Valley. Putting away the ledger, he startled at the raspy voice coming from a few feet away, surprised he hadn't seen the stranger enter the store.

"I need ammunition."

"Of course. What do you need?" Thomas stared at the man. He was certain he'd never seen him before. Close to six-foot-seven, as thin as a willow switch, he boasted a full mustache. It wasn't his height as much as his yellow eyes, rimmed in black with a black center, that had the store owner gawking. He found himself wondering what had caused the ragged scar running from his right temple to the tip of his chin. Thomas wisely held his tongue.

The man placed his revolver on the counter. "As many boxes as you've got."

"Nice gun." Thomas studied the .36 caliber weapon. "I've half a dozen boxes, with more expected on the next steamship."

"I'll take them all." He pulled money from his pocket, laying the amount Thomas quoted on the counter as the shop owner pulled boxes from the shelf behind him. "When does the next steamer come in?"

"Due on Sunday. I expect a dozen boxes of .36, along with other ammunition."

"I'll be back on Monday and will buy all you've got." Filling his arms, the man walked out, not sparing a glance to the three women who stepped aside, their mouths agape as he moved past them. When he closed the door, one of the women turned to Thomas.

"Who was that man?"

Thomas shook his head. "Never seen him before."

"He bought a good amount of ammunition." She glanced over her shoulder to see him walking across the street to the saloon. "Hope he's planning to ride out of town soon."

Thomas nodded. "So do I," he whispered, feeling a thick sense of unease settle over him.

Highlander Ranch
Saturday morning…

Geneen slid off Gypsy, the sorrel mare the MacLarens gave her not long after she arrived at Circle M with her sister, Sarah. She'd been riding an older gelding, one her father reluctantly passed on to her when the horse was too old to help around their farm. Although the horse made it from Oregon to Conviction, the long journey had taken a toll, prompting Ewan MacLaren to announce the animal might not make it through another winter.

Blaine and Fletcher MacLaren helped her train the three-year-old. Now Geneen couldn't imagine riding any other horse. As she walked Gypsy into the barn, she thought of the long rides she used to take with Nate, their talks, the laughter. She hadn't seen him laugh or smile for weeks before he rode away for the last time.

She'd hoped the memory of their shared experiences would have faded by now, stop haunting her from sunup to sunset each day. Instead, she found herself thinking of him more and more, wondering where he might be, if he'd found what he wanted, what she hadn't been able to give him. Colin's mother, Kyla, had told her many times his troubles had nothing to do with her, insisting Nate would find his way back to

Geneen when he put his demons to rest. Every night before falling asleep, she prayed Kyla was right.

"Such a good day." She turned to see Heather entering the barn, Caleb not far behind. Smiling at Geneen, Heather tied Shamrock next to Gypsy. "The cattle are moved to the north valley, and the horses are secure in the new pasture. And we've no need to prepare supper."

"How's that?" Caleb asked, stopping beside her with Jupiter.

"Mr. Beall said the ladies in town will be bringing enough food for an army. I asked what Geneen and I could bring, and he told us to enjoy the dance. Our turn to provide food would come soon enough."

"Which is good." Geneen removed Gypsy's saddle, placing it on a rack before grabbing a brush. "All I have energy for is taking a bath and dressing."

Caleb removed Jupiter's bridle, hanging it next to the horse's saddle. "When we left this morning, Archie said he'd put water on for baths."

"How wonderful!" Geneen offered a grateful smile. "Will he be going to town with us this evening?"

He led Jupiter out the back, setting him loose in the pasture before turning back to Geneen.

"Archie's staying here. Says he's been to more than enough dances." Caleb snickered, shaking his head, then sobered. "He told me he met his wife at a community dance over forty years ago. Said they were both older, neither of them thinking they'd ever marry. They made the trip west and ended up in Settlers Valley. She died a few years later during childbirth. He lost both her and the baby."

"How awful." Heather walked up to him, wrapping her arms around his waist. "He's never spoken of her to me."

"I doubt he talks about her much. Archie showed me a drawing someone did of her. It's old, wrinkled, and hard to make out, but I'm sure she was a real beauty." Caleb tightened his hold on his wife.

"Aunt Kyla says it's a risk having babies in the frontier. Worse when the mother is older." Geneen fiddled with a piece of rope, searching for something to pull them from the depressing subject. "Mr. Beall mentioned there's a doctor in town. Maybe he'll be at the dance and we can meet him. You know...just in case."

"Speaking of the dance, I'll be needing that bath soon. Geneen plans to do something with my hair." Heather patted the old, dust-covered hat she wore.

"Then we'd best get to it." Caleb kept his arm around her shoulders as they made their way to the house, glancing over his shoulder. "There might even be some unsuspecting lad at the dance who's perfect for Geneen. The same as Archie and his bride."

Laughing, she hurried up beside them. "It's not likely. I'll settle for a couple dances with men who don't step on my toes."

Heather gave her a smile. "You might not want to be setting your sights so high, lass. Not stepping on your toes is asking a lot."

The women were still laughing as they disappeared into the house.

Chapter Three

Nate sat on a bench in the shadows across from the church, watching people enter the community dance. The sounds of laughter and music greeted them as they walked inside. He knew no one would notice him with their attention focused on the revelry around them.

All he wanted was one long look at Geneen. Another memory to store away, along with the ones from the day Caleb and Heather married in the same church several weeks before.

A few times, he'd spotted her riding Gypsy in town, having no idea he hid at the back of the livery, watching. Most days, she secured her dark red hair at the back of her neck, a cowboy hat similar to what he wore covering the beautiful mane. The same as Heather, she wore pants and a man's shirt, ready for the hard work of a ranch hand.

Tonight, she'd be wearing a dress, and according to what he'd heard, a new hat from Beall's. Nate continued to watch the trail from the Highlander Ranch, hoping she hadn't changed her mind about attending.

A few minutes later, a wagon came down the road, three people on the bench seat. He didn't need to see them clearly to know they were Caleb,

Heather, and Geneen. His heart sped up as they approached, his breath hitching when he heard her laugh.

Caleb secured the line and jumped down, extending his arms for Heather, then Geneen. A ball of regret clogged Nate's throat. He should be the one escorting her inside. Instead, Caleb had the honor of ushering the two beautiful women out of the chilled night air and into the warmth of the festivities. Never had he envied a man more than he did his good friend.

As they entered, movement to the side of the church drew his gaze. Blinking a couple times, Nate leaned forward, attempting to get a better look at the darkened form. His eyes focused, revealing a tall, slender man wearing a black hat and long coat. A handkerchief covered his face, a gun in his right hand.

Fear pulsed through him as the man glanced around, stared up and down the street, then took a few tentative paces toward the front of the church. When he moved to the bottom of the steps, Nate stood, pushed aside his greatcoat, settling his right hand on the handle of his six-shooter, and began to walk quietly along the boardwalk toward the church. The man he watched looked around once more, apparently pleased with what he saw as he took the last few steps to the door. Nate's urgency increased as the man pushed the door open, his gun still in his hand, and stepped inside.

Running across the street, Nate heard a loud shout, then screams. As he came closer, the view through a window sent a chill down his spine. The man held the gun before him, motioning for people to move.

Nate shuddered, remembering a similar incident in Conviction when an armed group of men entered a dance with the hope of stripping the townsfolk of whatever valuables they had on them. The robbery had been stopped, but not before a Circle M neighbor, Quinn MacLaren's future father-in-law, was shot.

Looking through the window once more, Nate let out a relieved breath. The stranger had directed everyone to the other side of the room, leaving no one close to take as a hostage. All Nate had to do was get off one good shot, causing the man to drop his gun, and whatever he planned would be stopped.

Taking the steps slowly, he drew his gun, leveling it at the intruder. An instant before pulling the trigger, he froze as the barrel of a rifle dug into his back.

"Hold it right there, Hollis, and lower your gun." Sheriff Polk's rusty voice boomed through the slight opening in the church door, causing the intruder to freeze his actions and turn.

Before Nate had a chance to explain, the man barreled out the door, shoving Nate into the sheriff, causing both men to topple down the steps. Pushing up, Nate began to run after him.

"Stop right there, Hollis."

Turning, he saw the sheriff once again had his gun trained on him. "What the hell are you doing? The man's getting away."

The sheriff cocked his head, not lowering the gun. "What are you talking about?"

Nate had no chance to answer before a crowd of people surged from the building, surrounding them and shouting.

"Now you all quiet down. I have the man right here." The lawman pointed at Nate.

Marcus stormed up to him, fisted hands resting on his hips. "Dammit, Sheriff. That's not the man who wanted to rob us. That's Nate Hollis."

Even with the crowd, Nate could hear the gasp of disbelief, a muffled cry, and a deep-voiced curse coming from the top of the stairs. Turning, his gaze moved from Caleb to Heather, then finally to Geneen, whose face had gone ashen. Without a word, Caleb navigated down the steps, stopping in front of Nate.

"You've been here this whole time, Nate?" Caleb's low, angry voice was all the warning he got before his friend's fist connected with his jaw.

41

"How was I supposed to know Hollis was trying to help?"

The sheriff's protest broke through the haze of being knocked unconscious. Nate lifted his hand, rubbing his face where Caleb had struck him. Shaking his head to clear it, he opened his eyes. The first face he saw was Geneen's as she bent over him, her features drawn. Turning his head, he noticed Caleb beside her, not a bit of remorse on his face.

"You didn't need to hit me so hard, Caleb."

"I should've hit you harder." Extending a hand, Caleb helped him stand.

Looking down at the ground, Nate nodded. "You're probably right."

Marcus moved up beside Caleb. "You know Nate?"

Snorting, Caleb glared at his friend before glancing at Geneen and Heather, then back at Marcus. "All three of us do. He was a deputy in Conviction before he took off without a word to anyone." Caleb looked at Nate. "Isn't that right?"

He blew out a breath, not meeting Geneen's eyes. "Brodie knew. And I spoke with Kyla and Ewan before I left."

Geneen had heard enough. She threw up her hands, then poked a finger into his chest, her face taking on a red flush. "So you could tell Brodie, but not me?"

"Geneen, I—"

"After all the time we spent together, the suppers, the rides, me sitting by your bed when you were sick..." Her voice trailed off, her eyes moistening before taking on a hard glint. "You didn't see fit to at least let me know you were leaving?"

"Geneen, please, let me explain." He reached his hand out, meaning to touch her cheek.

Swatting his hand away, she shook her head. "How long have you been in Settlers Valley?"

"I—"

She stepped closer, poking his chest again. "Did you know I was in town?"

"If you'll—"

She held up her hand for him to stop, her eyes sparking. "If that man hadn't come into the church tonight, would you have ever let me know you were here?"

Staring down at his mud-encrusted, scuffed boots, he shook his head. "I don't know."

Her anger seemed to deflate at his confession, her shoulders sagging. "I see."

Nate barely heard her whispered response. The look on her face and agony in her eyes caused a tangible pain in his chest. He'd never meant to hurt her. Not ever. Her anguished features, broken voice, and ragged breathing told him he'd done just that.

He reached out to touch her hand, but she pulled away. "If you'll let me, I'll try to explain."

Lifting her chin, Geneen shook her head, straightening her spine. "Don't bother. I'm not daft, Nate. I understand what you're not telling me and why you felt no need to say a word about leaving. I'll do my best to stay out of your way if you'll do me the courtesy of the same." Turning, she rushed past Heather and Caleb.

He lifted his hand, trying to stop her, but she'd already moved out of his reach. "Geneen, wait."

The three watched as she reached the wagon and climbed onto the seat, her back rigid.

"Well, lad, you've made a fine mess of things."

Heather's words drew his gaze to her. "I never meant to hurt her."

"Nae. I think you knew what you'd be doing to her by riding off. That's why you never said a word. It was an awful thing you did to a fine woman."

Licking his lips, Nate closed his eyes, pinching the bridge of his nose. "She deserves better."

Heather slapped his arm. "The lass is wanting you, you eejit. She cares nothing about your injury or wounded pride."

Nate glared at her. "My wounded pride?"

"Aye, your pride, lad. What she sees is what the rest of us do. A fine lad, strong and honest. There would be nothing more she wants."

Nate dared a glance at Caleb, seeing the smirk on his friend's face. "Nothing more, you say?"

Caleb shook his head, as if Nate were the dumbest creature he'd ever seen.

Heather's voice softened. "You'd best be thinking this over, lad. I'd be guessing you'll be doing a good bit of groveling if you decide you want Geneen."

"I've always wanted her."

A wry smile curved up the corners of Heather's mouth. "Aye. A good bit of groveling."

It hadn't taken long for Sheriff Polk to let Nate go, never acknowledging he'd made a mistake in holding him instead of going after the true culprit. Instead, the sheriff issued him a warning about taking the law into his own hands. A warning Nate meant to ignore.

Caleb walked back up to him after seeing Heather to the wagon. "I'll be in town on Friday. We'll meet at the saloon, and don't think about telling me no. And do not even consider riding away this time. If you do, I'll personally come after you."

Nate would've laughed if he didn't know Caleb was serious. The MacLarens, and their extended family, never gave warnings they didn't intend to keep.

Staring at Geneen, who refused to look his way, Nate nodded. "Friday after work at the saloon."

Caleb studied him for a long moment before spinning around and returning to the wagon. Nate watched them take the trail to Highlander Ranch, his heart heavy, pain coursing through him. This time, it wasn't his arm throbbing. The anguish he felt lodged in his chest, choking him. Feeling a firm hand on his shoulder, Nate turned to see Marcus standing beside him.

"I've learned a great deal about you tonight, Hollis. Most of it good."

Nate struggled with how to respond. Marcus had been good to him, become a friend.

"I didn't do right by Geneen."

"I figured that much out, but I also figure you had your reasons for leaving."

Unconsciously rubbing his left arm, Nate nodded. "I did."

Marcus watched him, his gaze narrowing. "Do those reasons still exist?"

Blowing out a long breath, he shook his head. "I don't know. Maybe."

"I see." Marcus pursed his lips, struggling with what else to say. "I suggest you take some time and deal with what haunts you. She seems like a fine woman."

"The best."

"Then she deserves a man who's conquered his demons. You understand my meaning?"

"Yeah, Marcus. I do."

Chapter Four

Black Jolly paced in the abandoned shack several miles south of Settlers Valley, cursing himself. Knowing desperate men made bad decisions, he forced himself to calm down, think about his next moves and if they involved the small town north of him or another vulnerable spot.

Unlike his raids on Circle M several months before, he had no men to order about and little money. Once his benefactor, Giles Delacroix, crumbled under pressure, confessing his part in the crimes, Black had ridden at a grueling pace west, then north, and finally south again. He had no delusions about how easy he'd be to spot. His height, making him much taller than most men, and facial scar caused many men and most women to leave him alone. Still, if they'd seen the wanted poster Brodie MacLaren had sent out, there'd be few places he could hide.

Working with Delacroix had been a disaster. Black's men had either died or scattered. Money meant little to them when compared to the alternative of hanging or years spent in prison if they were caught. He didn't blame them. Black had no desire for either himself.

Reaching into his pockets, he emptied them onto a table, counting the remaining funds, noting he had enough for at least a month, more if he were careful. He had additional funds stashed in a Sacramento bank, money he'd saved for the woman who'd helped him in Conviction. She'd warned him to stop his scurrilous activities against the MacLarens and ride away, start over where no one knew him. Black pushed aside her pleas, as well as her offer to quit her job and come with him. Working with men was one thing. Having a woman in tow a different matter—one he had no intention of allowing.

For now, she didn't know where Black had gone, or that he'd backtracked to within a few hours' ride of her. He could check on her, make certain she was doing all right, without her knowing.

Right now, he needed more money. Trying to get it by robbing people at a community dance had been foolish. In his haste to take advantage of the joyous event, he'd almost been caught. If the sheriff's loud voice hadn't alerted him, Black would be sitting in a jail cell right now, planning his escape.

The one positive outcome of his trip into town came when spending an hour at the saloon. A group of Acorn miners didn't conceal their excitement about finding a new vein of gold. They'd toasted each other and played cards while Black listened. He'd heard of the Acorn Gold

Mine. Who hadn't in these parts? It didn't pay out as much as it had a few years before, but it still provided wealth for the owner and good wages for the workers.

He'd learned the discovery of the new deposit resulted in the owner giving his men the afternoon off. Listening, he learned the only ones still at the mine were a few guards, the owner, and his accountant.

After his failed attempt at the church, Black decided the mine would be his target. He just needed some time to study the operation, learn when the men came and went, and when they hauled the gold to town.

Most mines worked on a schedule, making the work more efficient and profitable, but also more attractive to men such as himself. Men who didn't care who had legal possession of what they wanted. In Black's mind, whoever carried it owned it. And that applied to gold.

Highlander Ranch

"You just can't be forgetting the lad's in town, Geneen. You'll be seeing him all the time."

Geneen stopped folding laundry, turning toward Heather. "Don't you think I understand

I'll have to see him? It's what's been keeping me up all week since the dance."

"A dance Nate kept from turning into a disaster. Who knows what would've happened if he hadn't seen that miscreant come into the church."

Dropping her hands to her sides, Geneen leaned against the table, a basket full of clean clothes on a chair beside it. "Caleb says he's been working for Marcus Kamm."

Heather nodded, lowering herself into another chair. "Aye. The lad's been working for him since before we arrived in Settlers Valley. Caleb suspects Nate's known we've been here all along. That's why he'll be going into town this afternoon. To find out what's in the lad's head."

Geneen shrugged, disappointment showing on her face and in the slump of her shoulders. "What does it matter? It's obvious Nate wants nothing to do with me."

"With any of us, lass."

Shaking her head, Geneen grabbed a pair of pants from the pile on the table, folding them before laying them on top of the stack in the basket.

"I don't think that's right. If I wasn't here, I'm sure he would've revealed himself to Caleb and you sooner. It's me he doesn't want any part of. He didn't even try to stop me from leaving town the night of the dance. Just let me ride off without explaining why he left."

Heather looked down at the folded hands in her lap, fighting the urge to smile. "I'm thinking you didn't give the lad a chance to explain. If I'm recalling right, he tried more than once, but you'd be having none of it."

Grabbing another chair, Geneen pulled it up to the kitchen table and sat down. Rubbing her face with both hands, she groaned. "You're right. He did try to explain. I just didn't want to hear his excuses. Not in front of all the townspeople who stood around, watching us."

They sat in silence for several moments before Heather cocked her head to the side. "Did something seem different about him?"

"How do you mean?"

"Think of how he looked before leaving Circle M. Skinny with sunken eyes and a sallow complexion. The lad moved sluggishly, not much faster than Archie."

Despite her despair, Geneen chuckled at the comparison.

"It's true, lass. Nate wasn't the lad we were used to seeing. But on Saturday night..." Heather's voice trailed off as she lifted a brow, looking at Geneen.

Catching her lower lip between her teeth, she tried to recollect his appearance. After a couple minutes, she nodded. "He did look more like himself. Healthy, with color in his face and a glint in his eyes." She swallowed the knot in her throat, meeting Heather's gaze. "Maybe he's met someone. A woman."

"You're jumping a wee bit ahead of yourself. There were no women around him, and none of those at the dance came running up to him. Nae. Maybe the lad's found a way to fight his need for the devil opium."

"If that's true, why didn't he come home? Come back to Conviction and the people who care about him?" Slamming a fist on the table, Geneen stood, crossing her arms. "It's because he no longer wants to be around me. Now that I'm here, he has every reason to return to his job as a deputy. Brodie wouldn't waste a second taking him back." Picking up the basket, she started for the stairs, glancing over her shoulder. "The man can jump into a cold lake with his clothes and boots on. Maybe they'll fill with water and I'll never have to worry about seeing him again..." Her voice trailed off as she pounded up the stairs.

"What's the matter with Geneen?" Caleb removed his hat as he walked in the back door, bending down to kiss Heather.

"I'll be giving you one guess."

He nodded, a knowing grin flashing across his face. "Nate."

"Aye. The lass is so angry, she might never forgive him. Assuming he wants to be forgiven."

"That's why I'm heading into town. I've some pretty hard questions for him." Setting his hat on a chair, he poured himself a glass of water, drinking it down in a few long gulps. "If you've a list, I'll stop at the general store."

"Nae. We're fine with what we have. Of course, if you're willing, you can ask Mr. Beall if he'll take back our hats. It seems a shame to have gotten only an hour of wearing out of them." The glint in her eyes told Caleb she was fooling...mostly. Although generous, Heather was also more frugal than most women.

"You'll have church on Sundays, Christmas Eve service, and other dances to wear the hats. You may not have had it on long, but you were beautiful." He pulled her up, wrapping his arms around her, kissing her soundly. After a few moments, she pushed on his chest, her breathing ragged.

"We've someone else in the house, Mr. Stewart."

"Someone who's seen us kissing before, Mrs. Stewart."

"You two can kiss all you want. I don't care at all."

Geneen's voice and the noise she made coming down the stairs had them pulling apart.

"I don't care at all who kisses who or for how long. I'm through with all of it." The front door opened, then slammed shut.

Glancing at each other, Heather began to laugh, Caleb following a few seconds later. Calming himself, he placed his arm over her shoulders.

"You're right. Geneen's not in her right mind when she's thinking of Nate."

Heather nodded, her face sobering. "Aye. The lass might never be in her right mind again."

Settlers Valley

Caleb rode straight for the livery. It never occurred to him Nate might have packed up and left. His friend wasn't a stupid man. He knew Caleb meant what he'd said about tracking him down. They'd never had a problem communicating.

Reining up outside the livery, he slid off Jupiter and strolled inside. Marcus worked at the forge, but he saw no sign of Nate.

"Good afternoon, Marcus."

The blacksmith looked up from his duties, straightening, not offering one of his soiled hands for Caleb to shake.

"Caleb. You looking for Nate?"

"I am."

"He's out back working on an order for Leland Nettles. Have you met the man?"

Caleb shook his head. "Can't say that I have. Who is he?"

"Owns the Acorn Gold Mine up the Feather River from your ranch. Ordered a new type of dredge for the operation. I'd been doing it all myself, but when Leland came in here demanding it be done sooner, I brought Nate in on it. He did such a good job, Leland ordered a second one." He wiped his soiled hands down the leather apron he wore. "Never met a man with so many talents as Nate, and so little belief in himself. He's got me stumped."

"Nate's got us all stumped, Marcus."

"From your conversation last Saturday night, I figure you must know him pretty well." He left the comment hanging between them, not wanting to push Caleb too much.

Taking off his hat, he wiped his brow. "Not as good as I once thought. He worked as a deputy for Brodie MacLaren, who wants him back wearing a badge in Conviction. Did a real fine job. You probably guessed he has a history with Geneen."

"I figured as much." Walking away from the forge, Marcus glanced at the door behind him, then back at Caleb. "Why'd he leave?"

"That's what I came into town to find out. Mind if I head back?"

"Head on out. It's time for him to finish up anyway." Marcus went right back to work, leaving the two men to their business.

Stepping out the back door, his gaze landed on Nate, who concentrated on a contraption Caleb had never seen before. His presence didn't go unnoticed long.

"Afternoon, Caleb." Nate set the dredge on the ground. "Didn't know if you'd ride in today."

He continued to study the device. "I said I would." Glancing up, he waited while Nate pulled off his gloves and grabbed his hat from a hook a few feet away. "Saloon?"

"It's as good a place as any for us to talk."

Caleb had no intention of pretending this visit overly friendly. Nate had hurt someone he cared about, a part of the MacLaren family, and he wanted answers.

"Let me clean up and I'll meet you out front." Nate headed to the back of the livery, washing his right hand in the trough near a small shack, then disappearing inside. He returned a couple minutes later wearing clean pants and shirt.

"You live in there?"

Nate's jaw worked, but he kept his voice smooth and even. "It comes with the job. A little smaller than the room I had at the Gold Dust in

57

Conviction. Marcus and I put in a new stove this week. Helps a lot." Nate walked ahead of him, cutting off further questions on the subject.

Making their way across the street, Caleb noticed new construction at the far end of town. "What's going in there?"

"I hear it's going to be a boardinghouse. The one we have has only three rooms for rent. This one will have eight. Thomas Beall at the general store is building it for his son, Percy, and his wife, Missy. He lost a leg in the war. Couldn't find work anywhere besides the general store."

Caleb could hear the bitterness in Nate's voice, but for now, he let it go. "Does he still work for Thomas?"

Nate nodded. "From what Marcus says, Percy and Missy will live in the boardinghouse. She'll cook and clean. Percy will help at the front desk and in the dining room, but will also work in the general store." He glanced at Caleb. "You do what you got to."

Again, he didn't comment, deciding it best to let them both settle with a glass of whiskey before asking questions.

Stepping into the Lucky Lady, the largest saloon in town, they found a table in a corner. Thanking the barmaid for the whiskeys, Caleb sat back, taking a slow sip before setting his glass down.

"How long have you worked for Marcus?"

"Since I got to town in early November." Nate rolled the glass between his fingers.

"Where'd you go after leaving Circle M?"

"San Francisco for a short time. Doc Tilden mentioned someone there who could help me."

Caleb didn't need to ask what he was talking about. "And did he?"

Leaning forward, he set his glass down, resting an arm on the table. "He said the same as Doc Tilden. The opium is out of my body."

Caleb cocked his head. "But?"

Shaking his head gently, Nate kept his gaze focused on the whiskey. "I still want it. As much as before. I wake up each morning and go to bed at night craving it. The doctor in San Francisco worked with me for several days, giving me ideas of what might help. The best suggestion was to find a place absent of opium. A town too small or remote to have it."

"That's how you ended up in Settlers Valley?"

Nate nodded. "I went through Yubaville, but there was no work." He mentioned the very small settlement just north of Conviction. "A bartender mentioned Settlers Valley." He shrugged, picking up the glass and draining it.

"How long have you known we were in the area?"

Lifting a hand, he signaled the saloon waitress for another round. "I saw Blaine, Quinn, and Heather ride into town one night. They came straight in here. I watched the entire scene from outside. It didn't take long to understand you'd finally gotten Heather to see things your way." A slight grin lifted the corners of his mouth.

"It wasn't easy. She's a stubborn lass."

"That she is." Nate lifted the refilled glass of whiskey, taking a sip. "A few days later, I saw other MacLarens ride in for the wedding."

"Were you at the church?" Caleb asked, sipping the whiskey.

Nate felt a rush of guilt. "Out of sight. I wasn't ready for anyone to see me." Leaning back, he looked at Caleb. "It was a fine wedding. Heather was beautiful."

Caleb nodded. "As was Geneen."

Ignoring the lump in his throat, Nate took another sip of his drink. "Yes, she was."

Caleb rubbed his chin as he studied his friend. "Do you love her?"

"Since the moment I saw her."

Stretching out his legs, Caleb tossed back the rest of his drink, crossing his arms. "You've some decisions to make."

Nate turned to face him, a brow lifting. "Such as?"

"How long you're willing to ignore your feelings for her. She's a beautiful, smart lass, and you're the man she wants."

Nate's jaw clenched, but he didn't respond.

"Some ranch hand is going to see what you let get away and claim her. Is that what you want?"

His nostrils flared. Again, he remained silent.

Caleb decided to change the subject. "Do you plan to stay in Settlers Valley, working for Marcus?"

Letting out a breath, Nate crossed his arms. "I haven't decided."

"Do you like the work?"

"It gives me a place to sleep, food in my stomach, and enough for an occasional whiskey."

"That's not what I asked. You're a good lawman, Nate, living in a town with an incompetent sheriff."

Chuckling, Nate nodded. "He's not looking for a deputy. Not that I've heard."

Caleb's gaze narrowed on him. "If he was, would you be interested?"

Sitting up straight, he glared at him. "Dammit, Caleb. Didn't you hear what I said earlier?"

Staying calm, he nodded. "Every word."

"Then you know I'm not fit to be a lawman, and definitely not fit for Geneen." Nate glanced around, seeing others watching him, and sunk back in the chair.

"What exactly did the San Francisco doctor tell you about dealing with the craving?"

"Work. Keep myself busy." He hesitated a moment. "Don't be alone," he breathed out.

Standing, Caleb stared down at him. "That's what I thought. Let's get out of here."

"Where are we going?" Nate's brows furrowed.

"We're picking up your belongings and I'm taking you to the ranch."

Chapter Five

It hadn't been a pleasant ride to Highlander Ranch.

Nate had adamantly refused to move his things to the ranch, insisting it was one of the worst ideas Caleb had ever uttered. He'd need to travel into town and back each day to continue work at the livery. This inconvenience accounted for little when compared to how Geneen would react.

Nate's warning had no effect on Caleb, who'd told him she'd learn to adjust. Nate continued to argue the point until his gaze met Caleb's cold stare and set features, seeing his friend's hands clenching and unclenching at his sides. For an instant, Nate wondered if Caleb would try to fight him. He didn't worry about getting hurt. His concern centered on what he might do to his friend. Even with one arm, Nate's fighting skills were well known by the MacLarens.

Caleb ignored all of Nate's cautions. The knowledge he'd be sharing a room in Archie's small house on the property made his concerns easier to accept, but didn't dispel them.

After a quarter-hour of arguing outside the livery, Nate gave up and stormed away, throwing his few belongings into saddlebags. He'd agreed to try Caleb's plan for one month, no longer, obtaining his friend's agreement Nate would be the one to make the decision as to whether he stayed at the ranch or moved back to town.

Trepidation at being so close to Geneen burned in his gut. Sweet-tempered and kind, he'd never seen her as angry and disappointed as she'd been when learning he lived in Settlers Valley. The warm, inviting smile he'd come to expect had been replaced with a deep anguish he hadn't anticipated. Nate knew he'd made a grave mistake not confiding in her before departing Circle M and leaving his job as Brodie's deputy. If he could do it over again, Nate would change many things.

After a brief explanation to Marcus, assuring his boss he'd still be at work each day, they rode off, saying little on their way to the ranch. The closer they got, the more Nate's gut churned. He knew the confrontation with Geneen wouldn't be pleasant. But he hadn't expected Heather's wrath at Caleb's invitation.

Stopping outside the barn, they dismounted, walking the horses inside to remove the tack. They'd not been home five minutes when Heather joined them, arms crossed as her gaze moved between the two, settling on Caleb.

"Are you daft, bringing Nate here with Geneen still in such a state?"

"Calm down, sweetheart. You'll understand once we've had a chance to talk. There are many things you don't know, but I'll explain all to you once Nate is settled. He'll be staying with Archie and riding to the livery each morning—not working the ranch with us."

She sucked in a deep breath before looking at Nate. "I'll be apologizing to you, Nate. It's just...I'm worried about Geneen. The lass has not been herself since seeing you in town."

He looked at Caleb. "As I said before, this is a mistake. I'll go back to town." Turning, he grabbed Nomad's reins, meaning to leave.

Walking to him, Heather placed a hand on his arm, stopping his movements. "Nae, you'll not be going. I trust Caleb when he says there are reasons you're here. Have you had supper?"

"No, but I don't expect to eat with you."

Her expression softened, a smile crossing her face. "We waited supper for Caleb. Now it will be including you. The lass may not be happy about it, but she needs to know what's been decided. There'll be no better time than tonight."

Letting out a ragged breath, Nate nodded. "If you're certain she'll be all right."

"I am. She's a gracious lass. There'll be no trouble."

Throwing up her hands, Geneen stormed across the kitchen, slamming a lid onto the warming stew. "Absolutely not. I'll not spend one minute sitting across the table from that man. Not ever."

"Caleb wouldn't be inviting him without good reason. You won't even be needing to speak to him. You'll just be needing to sit through supper, lass. Then you can leave."

Hearing the men enter the house, Geneen groaned. "I'll stay at the supper table one night, but that's all. And don't try to draw me into the conversation."

Heather looked at her, stifling a smile. "I'm not sure what you're meaning?"

Geneen didn't have a chance to answer before Caleb walked into the kitchen, putting an arm around Heather's shoulders before kissing her.

She pulled away, looking up at him. "And where's Nate?"

"In the parlor." He glanced at Geneen. "He wasn't sure it was safe to come in here with me."

Geneen shook her head, turning back to the stove. Removing the lid, she stirred the stew a few times. "It's ready." When she started to lift it, Caleb moved her aside, picking up the pot. "Fine. I'll bring the biscuits."

Caleb lifted a brow as he moved past Heather and into the dining room.

"The three of us will be talking as we always do, lass." Heather took down a basket, placing a towel inside before handing it to Geneen, who filled it with hot biscuits. "Nate can join in or not."

"I don't want to hear his excuses. Not tonight. Maybe not ever."

"Then we'll not be listening to any of it tonight. When we're done, Caleb will be helping me with the dishes. You go upstairs and forget the lad's even around."

Hugging her, Geneen gave Heather a grateful smile. "Thank you."

Lifting her chin, she held the basket with both hands and followed Heather into the dining room, ignoring Nate as she placed it on the table.

"Hello, Geneen." Nate's voice trembled enough to let her know he felt as uncomfortable as her. The knowledge gave her little satisfaction.

She glanced up. Nodding once, she moved to her place at the table. When he attempted to pull out the chair for her, she brushed him off and seated herself. Frowning, Nate walked to the other side, taking a place next to Caleb, who sat at the head of the table.

Without a word, Heather motioned for everyone to pass their plates. Once filled, they buttered their biscuits and dug in, no one saying a word for several minutes. Long enough for the room to fill with tension. After a while, Caleb set down his fork, looking at Geneen.

"Nate will be staying at the ranch, in the extra bedroom in Archie's house."

"That's what I hear." She didn't look at either Caleb or Nate.

"He'll be riding into town each morning to work at the livery, then returning in the evening. You'll need to plan on the four of us for breakfast and supper."

Nate shook his head, his gaze still locked on Geneen. "You don't have to do that, Caleb. I'll eat in town."

"Nae, lad. You'll be eating with us."

Geneen froze at Heather's words. They just agreed she'd sit with him at supper for just one night. Now she'd invited him to be present every night.

"You're still too thin, lad. You'll not be putting on weight eating whatever's been available in town."

"I usually ate beans."

"A lad needs more than beans to gain some weight. Am I right on that, Geneen?"

Feeling her throat tighten, she nodded, never looking up from the stew on her plate.

Caleb spoke up, doing his best to relieve the tension. "I've asked Nate to join us tomorrow."

"Ach. I'd forgotten we're hunting for deer." Heather set down her fork, looking at Nate. "It'll be good having one more shooter. We've plenty of beef and chicken, but it would be good to have venison for the winter."

Nate shook his head, his appetite not as strong as he thought. "I may not be of much help. It's been a long time since I hunted." He looked at Geneen, wondering if she remembered the hunt they went on with Quinn and his wife, Emma.

"We hunted with Quinn and Emma last winter." The words were out of Geneen's mouth before she could stop them.

"I didn't think you'd remember."

Pushing away her plate, Geneen stood, shoving her chair back in place. "Of course I remember. I remember everything, Nate." She looked at Heather and Caleb. "Excuse me." Walking from the room, all efforts at hiding her unease forgotten, she hurried up the stairs.

Heather stared at her empty place, a wry smile on her face. "The lass lasted longer than I thought she would."

"Maybe I should go talk to her." Nate slid his chair back and stood.

"Nae. Let her be for tonight. You need to give her some time."

"Do you think she'll ever forgive me?"

Heather glanced at the stairs, then back at Nate. "I don't know, lad. When she never heard from you, she decided to come with us."

"Why?"

"Her way of putting you behind her and starting over. When she's ready, she'll be talking to you." Heather stood, picking up plates before walking into the kitchen.

Caleb watched a series of emotions play across Nate's face, regret being the final one. It was an emotion he knew well. He'd felt the same when he believed Heather would never be within his grasp.

"It's a start, Nate."

He shook his head. "Not a very good one."

"It will get better each day. As Heather said, give her time." Standing, Caleb clasped him on the shoulder. "We're glad you're here. It's where you belong."

Lying in bed, Nate stared at the ceiling, not at all sure Caleb was right. He'd given Geneen enough pain and didn't relish the thought of giving her more. The not quite concealed anguish on her face told him everything. He'd hurt her deeply, more than he'd ever thought possible.

In Geneen, Nate had discovered a gentle soul, a woman who never uttered a bad word about anyone. She loved the outdoors, working the herd, hunting, and fishing. The same as Heather, Emma, and Coral, she could do all of it as well as most men.

Hunting with her the year before had been a sobering experience for him. The women he knew back east wouldn't have found any of it the least bit appealing. The fact he held a dangerous job as a deputy in a growing frontier town never bothered her. Neither had the loss of his arm. His reliance on opium hadn't made her turn away from him, disgusted with his need. She'd stayed by his side, doing her best to help him rid the drug from his body.

Geneen was the perfect woman for him. Except he'd left her behind, too afraid she'd see the real man and turn on him, just as his fiancée had. He still hadn't decided if a life with Geneen could happen. But he couldn't abide her hating him, not understanding his reasons for leaving. They might not sound logical or mean anything to her. All he knew was he had to try.

Heather and Caleb were right. Nate needed to give her time, let her get used to seeing him at the ranch, being back in her life. At some point, he felt certain she'd let him explain. Only then could they decide if she would forgive him, and if he could offer her a future.

Geneen sat on the window seat, staring at the foreman's house below. No doubt Archie was slumbering in his dark room. The second bedroom light still flickered. She wondered if Nate had found sleep illusive as well.

She'd stayed at the supper table as long as possible, doing her best to keep her gaze from wandering toward Nate's intense eyes. Leaving hadn't been her plan. Heather and Caleb expected her to be there and be courteous to Nate, even if she didn't join the conversation. Somehow, she knew they'd understand why she'd left and forgive her.

Taking the brush from her lap, Geneen took long, full strokes down her hair, letting it fall in waves over her shoulders and back. Nate had seen it down once—when he'd removed the pins from her hair as they lay beside the river on one of their rides.

They'd kissed for what seemed hours, bodies heating to an unbearable level. He'd stroked her back, pulling her close until their bodies aligned. She didn't know what she wanted. All Geneen knew was her body craved more.

Nate whispered to her as his lips traced a path down her neck, then back up. All the while, his hand moved over her, the dress she wore a slim barrier to the need pulsing through her.

When he pulled back, staring down into her eyes, she whimpered, not ready for him to stop.

Geneen continued brushing her hair, letting the memory wash over her.

Nate had continued to watch her, stroking his fingers down her cheeks, pressing more soft kisses to her mouth. She remembered protesting, asking if she'd done something wrong. He'd only shaken his head, telling her he'd never wanted a woman as much as he wanted her. Then comforting her by saying it wasn't the time. He'd told her no matter what her body and heart said, she wasn't ready. Nate hadn't stopped there. He assured her when they made love, she'd be ready, and there'd be no turning back.

Although they'd spent other long afternoons together, he'd never let it go as far as that one afternoon by the river. Geneen no longer wondered why. He simply hadn't wanted her enough—the same reason he'd left Circle M.

Geneen loved him with everything she had. It hadn't been enough. Someday she'd find the courage to allow him to explain his actions, but not now. She'd go through each day doing her chores, ignoring the fact the man she loved slept only a few feet away. It might as well have been a hundred miles. They were as far away from each other as they could ever be.

Chapter Six

Geneen hadn't bowed out of the hunting trip as Nate expected. By the time he entered the barn, she had Gypsy saddled.

"Good morning." He refused to ignore her, even though Nate suspected she'd prefer just that. Grabbing a halter, he walked to the back, opened the door, and whistled for Nomad. He stroked the gelding's neck before slipping on the halter and bringing him inside, seeing Heather and Caleb talking to Geneen. They quieted at his approach.

"How'd you sleep, Nate?" Caleb asked.

"Real good. I haven't slept in a regular bed in months."

Geneen looked at Caleb. She had no idea where Nate had been living, suspecting he'd taken a room at the boardinghouse she'd seen on the main street. He seemed in good spirits. Much better than she felt.

"Where are we headed?" Nate glanced over his shoulder at Caleb as he saddled Nomad, replacing the harness with the bridle, then mounted.

"About a half an hour north, past the Acorn Gold Mine. Archie says the deer are plentiful in the hills. There's a big lake up there, too." Caleb rolled up two oilskins, securing one behind his saddle, the other behind Nate's.

"Geneen and I packed food. We'll be having our dinner by the lake, and with luck, venison for supper."

Geneen's stomach clenched at Heather's statement, remembering all the times she and Nate had shared dinner along the river running through Circle M. Those days seemed so long in the past.

"Let's get started." Caleb reined Jupiter out of the barn, taking a trail behind the house that led them along the river. Heather followed behind him, then Geneen. Nate took up the rear, glancing around as they made their way north.

The Feather River ran through Conviction, bringing steamships loaded with passengers and supplies from Sacramento, continuing north to Yubaville before reaching Settlers Valley. Marcus had told Nate some made a couple more stops upriver, then turned around, while the majority headed back toward Sacramento.

His gaze moved to Geneen, who rode several feet ahead of him. She had a natural grace, sitting straight, yet relaxed in the saddle. Her movements were sparse as she guided Gypsy along the trail, staying a few yards behind Heather. Not once had she glanced back at him to make sure he still followed.

Not that he had anywhere else to go. If in town, he might've gone to church, taken a meal at the only restaurant, then found a seat on one of the benches on the boardwalk to watch the people move past.

Some Sundays, he rode south along the river, stopping once in a while to try his luck at catching a few fish. They were a welcome change from beans and the occasional batch of biscuits Esther would bring over. Although he never turned down any of the food she brought, his favorites were her fruit pies and cakes. The woman loved to cook, for which Nate was forever grateful. If staying at the ranch didn't work out, it wouldn't be at all hard to return to town and the tiny shack.

As he watched Geneen sway in the saddle, he found himself wanting to close the distance between them, both physically and emotionally. He couldn't stand the thought of their friendship dying because of his thoughtless and selfish actions.

A few miles along the river, Caleb led the group east into the foothills. Nate had never been this far north. The land boasted rolling terrain, low valleys, and ample grasslands. Over eggs this morning, Archie explained how he and his late wife had once thought of buying additional land up north, but then she'd passed away and he'd lost the heart to continue the dream.

From the little he'd seen, Nate saw nothing wrong with the spot Archie chose along the river for his ranch. Good grazing land, ample water, and a short ride to town, Nate thought it beautiful and the perfect place to raise a family.

His heart twisted. He'd once thought he'd have a family and several children by now. The war had torn his dreams from him. The odd part about it was he'd never been brokenhearted when his fiancée broke their engagement. In many ways, it had been a relief.

He'd envisioned the same kind of future with Geneen. Riding away from her had been excruciating, albeit necessary. He'd made progress since leaving Conviction and Circle M. Moving to the ranch might be the next step in making things right. If she ever gave him the chance, he'd explain his decision to her.

So lost in thought, Nate missed the others stopping along the trail, waiting for him.

"We'll split up here. Nate, you and Geneen take the trail to our right. Heather and I will take the left trail. The way the trails twist, Archie says we'll never be more than a quarter mile apart. It'll give us a better chance of finding deer."

"Wouldn't it be better to stay together our first trip, Caleb?" Geneen looked at Heather, hoping for support. "I mean, none of us have been up this way before. It might be safer if we didn't split up."

"Archie says it's pretty safe up this way. The occasional coyote or bear. He tells me the Indians are harmless."

"Indians?" Geneen arched a brow.

"There are several tribes up north. The ones we're most likely to encounter are the Nisanon, Kinkow, or Maidu. Archie's never had problems with any of them." Caleb glanced up the two trails. "They merge at the lake. We'll meet up again there."

"Wouldn't it be better if I rode with Heather, Caleb?" Geneen couldn't grasp the idea of spending a few hours hunting with Nate. She'd thought they'd all stay together, giving her the ability to keep her distance.

Caleb shook his head. "I want a man with each woman."

"It'll only be for a couple hours, Geneen. I'll do my best to stay out of your way."

Her heart hammered at the sound of Nate's voice a short distance away. She couldn't refuse, not without seeming churlish.

"You two ready?" Caleb moved his horse closer to Heather.

"As ready as I'll ever be."

Nate chuckled at Geneen's mumbled response. "We're ready. See you at the lake."

Moving up the trail, he stopped after several yards, shifting in the saddle to look at Geneen, who hadn't moved. "Are you coming?"

Geneen glanced at the retreating backs of Caleb and Heather, feeling trapped. Sucking in a frustrated breath, she guided Gypsy forward, not responding to Nate's question. The logic of Caleb's decision made sense. They came for deer and had a better chance of finding animals in two groups rather than one. Still, she didn't have to like the arrangements.

"We'll do the same as when we hunted with Quinn and Emma. Never get out of my sight."

"I remember," she hissed out, not wanting to listen.

"You'll need to stay close to me. Up here a ways, we'll dismount and walk the side trails. We might have better luck without the horses."

Geneen cringed at the thought of walking the trail with Nate. "We can split up when we dismount."

Reining Nomad up, he waited for her, noticing she took her time getting to him. "We stay together whether we're on or off the horses." He kept his voice reasonable, not wanting to anger her further. Geneen didn't have to come out and say how unhappy she was about riding with him. Nate could see it in her features, hear it in the tone of her voice.

"I know this isn't what you want, being forced to ride with me. We don't need to talk unless we get a kill. Until then, we can use the same hand signals we did with Quinn and Emma. All right?"

Pursing her lips, she looked away. "Fine."

He would've chuckled if he didn't know how much Geneen didn't want to be around him. He suspected she'd rather be anywhere else.

"Good. Let's go." Nate didn't wait for her response. They were losing time and he was determined to bring deer back to the ranch.

They'd been riding for less than fifteen minutes when crunching noises to their right had each stopping. Nate studied one side of the trail, Geneen the other, waiting for movement or sounds. It didn't take long for the rustling to begin again. Looking at each other, they slid from their horses, drawing rifles from their scabbards.

Nate signaled for her to follow him to the left. She shook her head, certain the noise had come from their right. Shrugging, he indicated for her to lead.

Ground tying Gypsy, Geneen moved off to the right. As they walked, the rustling continued, closer this time. Stopping, they stood still, careful to make no sound. A minute passed, then another as they looked around. Ahead of them, a large buck stepped into a clearing, followed a moment later by a second, smaller buck.

Nate breathed a relieved sigh, knowing they were downwind of the animals. They watched as the bucks lowered their heads, grazing on early winter grass. Catching Geneen's attention, he signaled for her to take the one on the left. He'd take the one on the right.

Slowly, each lifted their rifle and sighted. Nate took a quick glance at Geneen.

"Ready?" he whispered. When she made a slight nod, he sighted again. "Now."

Two shots rang out. Two bucks dropped to the ground. They had no time to celebrate. Running toward the fallen animals, they checked to see if they were just wounded. Both were clean kills.

"Great shot, Geneen."

Sparing him a slight glance, she nodded. "Yours, too."

Turning around, he whistled for Nomad. Both horses trotted toward them, stopping several feet away, reluctant to come closer to the fallen bucks.

"That didn't take long." Untying the oilskin, he rolled it out on the ground, then threw it across Nomad's back to protect the saddle.

Taking out a knife, he worked quickly to dress out each buck, then lifted them onto his horse, securing both with rope. He guessed them to be no more than seventy pounds apiece. Within twenty minutes, they were ready to leave.

He walked toward her, stopping when he heard two more shots. Nate looked at Geneen and smiled. Amazingly, she returned a small one of her own.

"We'll both need to ride Gypsy."

Geneen nodded, knowing she had no other choice unless she wanted to walk. Mounting, she waited for Nate to swing up behind her. When she felt his arm slide around her waist, she sucked in a breath, shoving aside the warmth his touch created. Doing her best to ignore the man behind her, she clucked for Gypsy to move.

"We need to talk about my reasons for leaving, Geneen."

Nate's arm tightened around her waist, his warm breath against her skin causing her stomach to churn. Her body reacted to him in complete contradiction to what her mind told it to do. When she didn't respond, he continued.

"I had to go, and you need to know why."

She let Gypsy continue along the trail, closing her eyes for an instant to calm the raging desire his closeness created. Sitting straighter, she tried to create some distance between them. He'd have none of it. His arm tightened around her a little more.

"I'm sorry for leaving without telling you. If I could do it over, I'd handle it in a different manner."

Letting out a breath, she shifted, looking over her shoulder. "It's quite simple, Nate. If I'd meant enough to you, I doubt you would've considered leaving without explaining your reasons. You would've given me the courtesy of a goodbye."

"It wasn't that simple, Geneen."

She shook her head, frustrated with his lack of understanding. "Perhaps not to you, but to me, it was. You took time to tell Brodie and quit your job. You met with Kyla and Ewan. I assume you explained your reasons to them."

He hesitated a moment before answering. "You're right. I did explain. All three needed to know. Brodie because he was my boss, and Kyla and Ewan because they'd done so much to help me rid my body of opium."

"While I sat around day and night doing nothing, right?"

He felt the blood rush to his face. "No, that's not right. I'm handling this all wrong."

She glanced back at the trail before looking over her shoulder again. "Because there is no right explanation. If you cared about me as much as I did you, nothing could've stopped you from explaining why you had to go." Her voice rose with each sentence, her heart hammering in her chest.

"That...isn't true." He stumbled over the words, wondering if there might be a seed of truth in what she said. He'd been in love with her, hadn't he?

"Of course it is." She saw the lake ahead, slowing their pace. "I believe you cared about me, but weren't in love with me. While you rested in bed, you had a great deal of time to consider the two of us, and I think you came to realize I'm not the right woman for you. The easiest way to break it off was to leave. Ride out without telling me."

"You make it sound as if I planned to hurt you."

Reining to a stop next to the water, she felt her body begin to shake as anger took control. "No. I believe you were never in love with me, so explaining your reasons wasn't important." She let out a ragged breath, tired of going in circles with him. "Whatever I thought we had was a fantasy, a dream I harbored in my mind. You never had the same dream. I understand that now and beg you to leave it alone."

Nate loosened his hold, refusing to drop his arms. "You're wrong about so many things. If you'd give me some time, I can explain all of it."

Looking around, she saw Caleb and Heather riding toward them. "Not now. Not this week, and maybe never. I don't want to waste my time listening to you rationalize something that can't be undone. You've moved on, and so have I."

Ignoring the approaching riders, he tightened his arm around her, pulling her close. Leaning down, he placed a kiss on her neck, feeling her shiver.

"Have you moved on, Geneen? Your reaction to me says otherwise." Nate gave her a moment to think about his words, then slid to the ground, watching her chest heave. She was still angry and hurt, but not indifferent to him, as she wanted him to believe. She couldn't push him away forever. It would take time. Thank goodness he had plenty of it to spare.

"We'll be riding to the ranch with four deer." Heather's excited voice broke through his thoughts, returning to the reason for them being at the lake.

"We'll need to hang them in the trees while we eat." Caleb began to loosen the ropes around the deer secured on Jupiter's back while Nate did the same to the ones on Nomad's. "They aren't very big animals, but they'll provide us with enough venison to give us a change from beef, pork, and chicken."

After hanging the deer from branches, Nate walked over to where Geneen placed the food on a blanket. Leaning down, he lowered his voice so no one else heard. "This discussion is far from over. Don't think I'm giving up on us."

Her breath caught. She had no more to say to Nate. If he wanted to believe otherwise, so be it. She'd made her decision. She meant to push him from her heart and move on.

After eating with haste, they packed up, mounted their horses, and were about to leave when the sound of men's voices stopped them. Hands resting on their guns, the four waited.

An instant later, an Indian boy, perhaps twelve years old, crashed through the bushes, coming to a stop several feet away when he spotted them. Eyes wide with panic, he shifted from one foot to the other, searching for a means of escape. When the men's shouts grew closer, his body tensed as he turned toward the voices, the knife in his hand rising into the air.

Nate and Caleb slid from their horses, holding up their hands as they walked toward the boy. Neither made a move to pull their guns, doing their best to show him they meant no harm.

"There he is." The high-pitched screech had Caleb and Nate moving in front of the boy at the same time a group of men appeared from out of the bushes. The one in the lead pointed to the boy. "You there. Grab him."

They made no move to detain him.

"Move aside."

Nate took a step forward. "What do you want with him?"

"He killed a man at the mine. We're taking him back to hang."

His gaze narrowing on the man who appeared to be their leader, Nate's hand moved to rest on the butt of his gun. "You saw him kill the man?"

"Don't matter. We all know he's the one that done it." The men began to raise their rifles.

"I wouldn't do that, gentlemen." Nate looked toward Geneen and Heather, seeing each of them holding rifles, aiming at the group of men. "See those women over there?"

Several of the men glanced toward them.

"They're both good shots. Hardly miss. And from this range, well...all I can say is I wouldn't do anything to make them pull the trigger." By the time his words were out, Nate had slid his six-shooter from the holster, the same as Caleb.

The leader's face reddened. "You can't protect that boy. He's a murderer."

"So you say. Last I heard, he should be arrested and put on trial in Settlers Valley. We're headed back that way now and will be glad to deliver him to the sheriff." Nate held the gun steady at his side, hoping they didn't push him to use it.

"Sheriff Polk don't give a whit about an Indian. He'll do whatever Mr. Nettles says, and I'm letting you know, the boss is going to order him to hang the Indian."

Nate's jaw tightened. He believed the sheriff incompetent, but wouldn't have guessed him to be beholding to Leland Nettles.

"Nevertheless, the boy goes with us. I'd suggest you all go back to the mine and let your boss know what happened."

A feral grin appeared on the man's face, his teeth crooked and yellowed. "You've no idea the trouble you're bringing on yourself."

"You tell him to speak with Nate Hollis at the livery. He knows who I am."

The man shook his head. "Don't say I didn't give you fair warning." He looked over his shoulder at his men. "Put your guns down. We need to get back and let the boss know what happened." He glared at the Indian, then settled his gaze on Nate one more time. "If you was a smart man, you'd be leaving the Indian with Polk, then riding out of town. Mr. Nettles isn't going to take kindly to you siding with Indians."

The corners of Nate's mouth tilted up into a wry grin. "Probably not, but that's the way it's going to be."

They waited until the group of men disappeared into the forest before sliding their guns back into their holsters, Geneen and Heather putting the rifles into the scabbards. When Nate turned around, the boy had disappeared.

Chapter Seven

Archie scratched his chin, his gaze focused into the distance. "From the way you describe him, I think the boy might be from the Maidu tribe. I've never had any problem with them and never heard of them killing anyone. Most times, it's the whites going after them."

Nate, Caleb, Geneen, and Heather worked around a large table out back of the main house, preparing the venison to be smoked, dried, or canned, while sharing the story of the Indian boy.

"Do you think he could've killed one of the miners?" Geneen asked.

Archie looked up from where he worked next to Caleb. "Doubtful. It's more likely one of the other miners killed the man." He set down his knife, wiping his brow with a handkerchief. "The Maidu do their best to stay out of the way of the whites. They're a small tribe, less than a thousand. Their villages are spread throughout the valleys and mountains around here. I'm guessing less than fifty or sixty people live in each. They gather what they can and hunt. Can't say as I've ever seen any of them on a horse, but they might have them. You say the boy was about twelve?"

Geneen nodded. "He appeared to be, but he could've been ten or fourteen. The only weapon I could see was the small knife he held in his hand."

"It seemed the right size to kill a small animal or bone out a fish." Nate's mouth twisted. "I didn't ask how their man died."

Geneen's eyes widened. "I didn't see any blood on his knife. Wouldn't there have been blood if he'd killed a man?"

"He could've wiped it clean." Caleb set the meat he'd prepared in a bucket, then moved to the next animal. "I wish he hadn't run off before we had a chance to talk to him."

Archie chuckled, shaking his head. "I doubt he speaks English. Like I said, they stay as far away from the whites as they can. A few of them speak some broken English, and no white man I know speaks any Maidu." Wiping his brow again, Archie looked at Nate. "Leland Nettles is a bad-tempered man. Thinks because he owns a prosperous mine he can get away with whatever he wants."

Nate rinsed his right hand in a bucket of water, drying it on a towel. "What are you saying?"

"Those men were right. Sheriff Polk will do whatever Leland tells him. It's a good thing the boy took off. You don't want to get in the middle of anything going on at the Acorn."

Geneen waited until Nate moved away from the table before washing her hands. She'd been near him all day, fighting her strong desire and schooling herself not to be swept up in her feelings for him. Working around him on the ranch could work, as long as he stayed in town most days. It would be the times they were alone she had to be wary about. For the first time since coming to Settlers Valley, she wondered if the time had come to return to Circle M.

"I'd better head inside and start supper."

Heather stopped working, looking over at her. "Will you be needing help?"

"No. You go ahead and finish up out here. Supper will be a simple meal tonight." Heading up the steps, she didn't look behind her to see Nate's gaze following her.

Geneen sat at the table, staring at the empty place where she'd expected Nate to be sitting. He'd told Caleb and Heather he'd be eating with Archie tonight in the foreman's house. She couldn't help thinking it was his way of putting distance between them.

Their earlier conversation hadn't been pleasant. He'd done all he could to persuade her to let him explain his actions. The piercing pain of him leaving prevented her from allowing him the chance to hurt her again. The fact she felt such acute disappointment at him choosing to eat with Archie over her confirmed she'd made the right decision in pushing him away.

"Archie wanted to speak with Nate more about the locals, particularly Sheriff Polk and Leland Nettles."

Geneen looked up to see Caleb watching her. "I'm sorry. Were you speaking to me?"

"I was." Chuckling, he picked up his cup of coffee and took a sip. "You already know Archie's been around here since before most everyone else. His body might be betraying him, but his mind is still sharp. He's worried about Nate coming up against Polk and Nettles. Working in town at the livery makes him an easy target for them. Us protecting the Indian boy didn't help."

"You did what was right, Caleb."

"Nate and I believe that, Geneen, but Nettles won't see it the same way. Wouldn't surprise me if he rides into town tomorrow to confront Nate, and he'll have Polk beside him when he does it."

"I'm wishing we had a lad like Brodie in Settlers Valley."

"Or Nate."

The women cast surprised looks at Caleb. Geneen responded first.

"Has Nate mentioned taking over Polk's job?"

"Not a word. I'm just saying he'd be a darn good sheriff and wouldn't let Nettles buy him off the way Polk does."

"Aye. Nate wouldn't be allowing Nettles to get away with all he does. Polk is old and set in his ways." Heather's lips twisted into a sneer. "And lazy. Maybe he'll be deciding to retire and Nate can be taking his place."

"If he doesn't leave."

Caleb's startled expression locked on her. "Did he say something about leaving, Geneen?"

"No, but it seems it's his way of dealing with life. When bad things happen, he takes off rather than face them directly."

"I'm sure the lad had his reasons, lass." Heather's words were gentle. "Did he speak of them to you today?"

Geneen felt a pang of guilt, knowing she had shut him out when he'd tried to get her to listen. "No. What's done is done, Heather. Words matter little when it's actions that tell the story." Pushing her chair away from the table, she stood, reaching for their empty plates.

"I'll be cleaning up, lass."

Letting out a weary sigh, Geneen nodded. "Thanks, Heather. I'll be heading to bed then."

Taking the stairs, she couldn't help her thoughts from wandering to Nate, the feel of him behind her as they rode to the lake. So much about him felt right. Too bad he was so wrong for her.

Nate woke early, saddling Nomad for the ride to town. He wanted to arrive at the livery before Marcus and finish the second dredge Leland ordered. If there were to be ramifications for his actions regarding the Indian boy, Nate didn't want any backlash against his boss. He also intended to get away from the ranch before the others started their day. Especially Geneen.

She'd been adamant about not wanting to hear his reasons for leaving. The more he thought on it, the more it made sense to ignore what happened and move on. He found himself fighting a constant battle between his heart and mind.

One told him she was the one woman who could help him heal, help him deal with the torment of the past few years. The other reminded him of how much he still craved the relief opium brought him. But it came at a cost. One he didn't want her to endure.

He hadn't taken the drug in weeks. Being unavailable in Settlers Valley made staying in the small town appealing. Returning to Conviction, as he'd once anticipated, meant facing the temptation on a daily basis. A challenge he didn't feel ready to accept just yet.

The sun broke over the eastern hills as he entered the outskirts of town. Few people were about, most still rubbing the sleep from their eyes. Sliding off Nomad, he walked him through the gate into the back of the livery, removed the saddle and tack, then began work on the dredge. If he had few interruptions, he'd have the device done by the time he left for the day.

"I didn't expect to see you here so early."

Nate didn't glance up at Marcus's comment, keeping his focus on the dredge. "I want to finish this up for Nettles."

Marcus leaned against a post, crossing his arms as he watched Nate work. "He won't be sending a man to get it until Wednesday."

"Do you have work for me after this is finished?" Nate continued working on the dredge, inspired to finish it.

Marcus chuckled. "There's enough work for three men for weeks." He didn't budge from his spot against the post as he studied Nate. "All going well at the ranch?"

Stilling, Nate straightened, setting down the tool he'd been using. "As well as you might expect."

"Miss MacGregor seems like a fine woman."

Nate's jaw clenched. He didn't want to speak about Geneen to anyone. "She is," he ground out, picking up the tool and turning so his back faced Marcus.

"Men are lining up now that they know she's got no man courting her."

This time, the tool slid from his grip, dropping into the dirt. His hand clenching at his side, he looked at his boss. "What do you mean?"

Shrugging, Marcus pushed away from the post. "Nothing much. Had a few of the single men come by last week, asking if I knew her and if she was single."

"What did you tell them?"

"They'd have to speak with Caleb Stewart...or you."

Mumbling a curse, Nate bent to pick up the tool. "She's not mine, Marcus."

"If that's true, it shouldn't matter if other men show an interest. Truth is, if I was half as good as she deserved, I'd be talking to Caleb myself. Good thing I'm a man who knows my limits." Stepping next to Nate, he clasped his shoulder. "You'd best make sure what you're willing to give up. There may come a time you can't get her back."

Nate felt Marcus's warning spike straight down to the tips of his boots. He just needed time to figure out what to do with it.

Acorn Gold Mine

Black Jolly held the field glasses still, watching Leland Nettles take out his temper on a group of hired men. They stood ramrod straight, flinching every few seconds as the words tumbled out of their boss's mouth. Black couldn't hear what was said, but he'd swear it had to do with the miner he'd killed the day before.

And the young Indian he'd seen fleeing through the woods an hour later when the boy stumbled on the miner's body while tracking game.

Black should've done a better job of hiding the body, taken more time and dug a deeper grave. After dragging the lifeless form yards behind the guard shack, he'd carved out a few inches of dirt, laid the body into the shallow hole, then covered it with leaves.

The risk he took going down into the camp instead of staying on high ground and watching had been worth it. The cocky guard had been privy to much more than Black expected. He now knew the schedule Leland used to transfer the gold to town, how many men rode along, how they were armed, and the approximate value of each shipment. Black didn't need a full wagonload. Just enough to stuff his saddlebags. And he'd need his own men.

He didn't know what happened to the Indian and didn't care. A group of miners had spotted the boy bending over the conspicuous mound. Their shouts scared him away. Black waited behind a copse of trees as the boy ran off. The group stopped briefly to see what lay below the leaves, then took off yelling, their guns drawn.

Black hadn't even considered following. He didn't give a whit about what happened to the Indian. If he escaped, fine. If not, it made no difference what they did to the boy.

He had one goal in mind as he took a long, circuitous path around the miner. Black needed men and he needed them soon.

Geneen worked through the day, telling herself she didn't care about Nate not showing for supper the night before or breakfast this morning. Caleb had seen him ride off not long before sunrise. An hour after sunset, he still hadn't returned.

"What's for supper? Smells good." As usual, Caleb came through the back door, leaving his soiled boots by the door before entering the kitchen.

"Venison. I took some before we started curing the meat. We should have several meals off it." Geneen turned back to the frying pan on the stove. "Potatoes and biscuits are ready. By the time you get cleaned up, the venison cutlets will be on the table. I plan to roast one of the legs tomorrow."

"I haven't had roasted venison in a long time."

Geneen startled at Nate's voice coming from behind her. Shifting around, her stomach twisted at the sight he made leaning against the doorframe, his legs crossed.

"I didn't know if you'd be joining us." She did her best to make the comment casual, as if she didn't care either way. The slight tick in his cheek indicated she may not have succeeded.

He pushed off the doorframe, taking a few steps toward her. "What are you serving with the venison tomorrow night?"

Clearing her throat, she turned back to the pan on the stove. "I'll roast potatoes. We've also some carrots and turnips."

"Those would be real good with the roast."

Caleb listened to the interchange, Nate's voice low and calm, Geneen's shaky and stilted. Shaking his head, he moved past them. "I'd best leave you two to your conversation while I clean up." He walked out of the kitchen, a smirk firmly in place.

Stepping behind her, Nate rested his right hand on Geneen's waist, feeling her body stiffen. Glancing over her shoulder, he breathed in the aroma of frying meat mixed with her distinct scent. He'd never forget how she felt in his arms or his body's reaction to the smell of rosewater and lavender wafting off her skin.

Leaning down, he brushed a kiss along her neck, then stepped away, but not before feeling her tremble. "I'll leave you to finish. Unless you need my help."

"No...no...I'm, uh...fine on my own."

Before leaving the room, Nate took one quick glance over his shoulder, a slight grin crossing his face at the sight of her hands shaking.

Geneen waited until his footsteps receded before letting out the breath she'd been holding, her shoulders sagging. The wrought iron spatula shook in her hand as she turned the cutlets. She didn't want to feel anything, especially desire, for the man who'd broken her heart.

Grabbing a platter, she slipped the cutlets into the center, piling boiled potatoes around the sides. When she tried to turn around, her legs felt weighted to the floor, her mind unable to control her movements. Setting the platter down, she rested her hands on the counter, lowering her head. Taking deep breaths, she willed her heart to calm and the tightness in her chest to ease. She'd never been good at hiding her feelings and couldn't go into the dining room feeling the tension flowing off her. Heather and Caleb would notice it. Worse, so would Nate.

"How are you doing, lass?" Heather came to stand beside her. "Looks grand. May I carry it to the table?"

"Yes, please." She picked up the platter, shoving it at Heather.

"Are you feeling all right?"

"Fine. A little tired from the hunt yesterday and all the work today."

Heather's gaze narrowed on Geneen, studying her features. "I'm not believing it, but am sure you'll be telling me when you're ready."

When she left the room, Geneen debated whether to join them or make an excuse and go to her room. Her appetite no longer tugged at her as it had before Nate appeared, the hunger disappearing as fast as Nate after he'd set her body on fire.

Fighting the urge to disappear, she straightened her back, letting her arms hang loose at her sides, and left the kitchen. Heather sat in her usual place. Nate stood behind Geneen's chair. Without a word, he pulled it out, making certain she was settled before walking around the table to take his own seat.

"What a grand idea to have the cutlets tonight." Heather took the platter from Caleb, taking some venison and potatoes before passing it to Geneen. "Caleb says you'll be making roast tomorrow."

Geneen knew someone spoke to her, but she couldn't quite register who with her gaze locked on Nate. Her breath caught, stomach tilting as she forced herself to look away, but not before she saw the barely contained desire in his eyes.

Chapter Eight

Conviction

Brodie stared down at the letter from Caleb. He'd read it twice. The first time in disbelief, the second to squelch the anger he felt at Nate being so close to them all these months.

He read it through a third time, making certain not to miss a single detail. Finishing all four pages, he began to understand his friend's motives for leaving—at least through Caleb's eyes. Brodie wanted to understand by speaking to Nate himself. Setting down the letter, he glanced up as the door to the jail opened.

"A crowd is gathering near Chinatown." Brodie's brother-in-law and deputy, Sam Covington, walked in, taking a seat on the other side of the desk. "Jack and Seth are keeping order."

Jack Perkins, Seth Montero, and Alex Campbell were the three other deputies. He'd hired the last two after Nate left. Brodie still needed one more, but lacked the motivation to look, hoping his friend would return to resume his duties.

"What is it this time?"

"A woman new to town went into one of the Chinese stores to get medicine for an ailment. Her husband claims she died from what they gave her. He's quite vocal about his desire to close the store and similar ones."

Brodie steepled his fingers under his chin. "Was she examined by Doc Vickery or Doc Tilden?"

Sam nodded. "Doc Vickery. He couldn't find evidence whatever she bought killed her. Doc's seen her a couple times since she and her husband arrived by steamship a month ago. He told me her heart was failing. She didn't have long to live. Probably why she sought out something that might help."

"Aye, it probably is. Her husband is grieving, directing his anger at those he believes are responsible."

"August Fielder arrived before I left. He thinks the crowd will disperse after they've had a chance to voice their anger."

"What do you think, Sam?"

Rubbing his chin, he pursed his lips. "I'm not certain. That's why I left Jack and Seth to make sure no violence broke out."

"Where's Alex?"

"He rode out this morning to check on a report of missing cattle. I doubt he'll be gone long." Sam looked over his shoulder when the door opened, seeing Seth walking in. Removing his hat, he took a seat next to Sam.

"What of the crowd?" Brodie asked.

"Doc Vickery showed up and took the husband aside. It didn't take long for people to leave." Seth stretched out his long legs, crossing his arms. "Jack's getting breakfast at the Gold Dust. Is there anything you need me to do, Sheriff?"

"Be at the docks when the steamship comes in today." Brodie debated whether or not to say anything about Nate in front of Seth. They'd never met, so he doubted Seth would care one way or another what happened to the man. Seth made the decision for him. Standing, he settled the hat on his head.

"Guess I'll join Jack at the Gold Dust before heading to the docks."

When the door closed, Brodie picked up the letter, sliding it across the desk to Sam. "Read it."

Sam's eyes widened as he read what Caleb wrote. "I'll be. Nate's been a few hours up the river all this time and never let anyone know. Son of a..." He didn't finish, shaking his head as he passed the letter back to Brodie. "Must have been quite a shock for Geneen."

"Aye, it must've. I'm thinking of riding up there to talk to Nate. Maybe there's something I can do to get him back here."

"Caleb says Nate told him he picked Settlers Valley because opium isn't available like it is here. You know we can't control the stuff. As hard as it is to say, maybe it's best he not come back to Conviction."

Standing, Brodie paced to the window, looking out at a street already crowded with wagons and horses. "You may be right. I hate to think of the lad hiding out when there might be something more we can do."

"He's got Caleb, Heather, and Geneen close by. And Caleb mentioned trying to talk him into living at the ranch. Being closer to friends might be all he needs right now."

"Aye, you're probably right."

"You're needed here, Brodie. I know it's just a few hours away, but if anyone should go, it's me. With Maggie pregnant, you don't want to be too far away."

"The lass isn't due for a while yet, Sam."

Joining him at the window, Sam clasped a hand on Brodie's shoulder. "Reply to Caleb. Let him know one of us can ride up there if he thinks it's needed. Nate left because he felt he had to. Whatever he's doing seems to be working."

Brodie turned toward him. "He's a good lawman working in a livery."

Sam chuckled at the thought. "It's honest work."

"Aye, it is."

"I'd best start my rounds. Jinny expects me to be home for dinner." Sam patted his stomach. "She's a real good cook."

"Of course she is. Our mother taught her well."

Brodie watched Sam walk out, still unsettled by the news about Nate. He told himself Sam was right. His friend was doing what he thought best. It wasn't Brodie's place to try to convince him otherwise.

Returning to his desk, he penned a short letter to Caleb.

Settlers Valley

Black sat at a table in the Lucky Lady, his back to the wall, as far away from the entry as possible. It might not be the best day to find men willing to ride with him, but he couldn't wait any longer. The load from the Acorn would be transported to town next week. It could be as long as three weeks before the next shipment, too long for Black to wait.

"The bartender said you're looking for men." A man of average height stood across the table, his expression sullen, hands twitching at his sides. "What kind of work do you have?"

Black's expression didn't change as he studied the man. He could afford to be a little picky, but not much. "You good with a gun?"

The man lifted a brow, nodding. "Good as the next."

"Are you willing to use it?"

The man's gaze narrowed. "On what?"

"Other men."

"I'm no killer. Just looking for work."

"Then I think you'd best keep looking." Black looked down at his whiskey, dismissing the man. One man had already been hired. He only needed one more.

He'd spent two days forming his plan before riding back to the mining camp, requesting a meeting with Nettles. At first, he'd been rebuffed. When he mentioned word was out about when the next shipments would be made, he'd been ushered inside.

Black used his time wisely, explaining the dangers of moving gold from place to place. The mine had been lucky so far. Black hinted the killing of the guard could've been by the Indian boy, or it could've been by someone else—men not averse to robbing from their employers. Black provided a list of people he'd worked for, impressing Nettles. The outcome was always the same. He'd offer up the names of prominent people he didn't know, but seldom did anyone take the time to check his association with those on the list. It amazed him how the right name could open doors anywhere.

It hadn't taken too much persuading for Nettles to hire him to guard the shipments. Black's only request was that he use his own men. Nettles had agreed, asking few questions.

Being an employee of the mine gave him access to a good deal of information, and kept the sheriff away. As someone taking money from Nettles, Polk had little reason to question Black, looking away while he conducted his interviews at the Lucky Lady. If any of the men he didn't hire went to Polk, the sheriff would brush their comments aside, thinking Black was hiring guards. Men who wouldn't care about shooting a man if he tried to steal the contents in the wagon. Black had it all covered.

"Bartender says you're hiring."

Black glanced up. It had become a familiar comment the last two nights. This time, Black's brow lifted in interest. The man had a promising look about him.

"Have a seat." He slid an empty glass and bottle of whiskey toward the man, who didn't hesitate to accept. Leaning back in the chair, he waited until the man poured a drink and tossed it back.

"What kind of work are you offering?"

"Depends. Do you have any objections to shooting a man?"

He shook his head. "Not if it needs to be done."

Black studied him another moment, then leaned forward, resting his arms on the table.

"I need guards for a shipment from a local mine to town."

Shrugging, the man cocked his head. "Seems easy enough. When?"

"Next week. I'll let you know the day before I need you. Where are you staying?"

"At the boardinghouse. I got the last of her three rooms." Standing, the man offered his hand. "Colt Dye."

"Black Jolly."

Colt nodded. "I'll wait to hear from you." Strolling out of the saloon, he took one quick glance over his shoulder at Jolly before heading down the boardwalk.

Sitting down, Black poured another drink. He had his two men. If all went well, late next week he'd be several hundred miles away and a good deal richer.

Colt settled himself into a seat at the boardinghouse supper table, eyeing the other two renters. They'd been introduced as a traveling salesman and a young man who described himself as a fledgling photographer.

"And what do you do, Mr. Dye?" Dahlia Keach, the matronly widow who owned the establishment, sipped her tea, glancing over the rim as she waited for his answer.

Colt set down his cup, threading his fingers together in his lap. "I've done many things, Mrs. Keach."

"Well then, what is your most recent line of work?"

He knew the woman would continue asking until he answered.

"I worked for a group of ranchers in Texas as an investigator." It might not be the complete truth, but it wasn't a lie.

Her eyes lit up. "How interesting. My late husband did some investigation work when we lived in Chicago...after he retired from the police force. He quite enjoyed it. In fact..."

Colt let out a breath, pleased he'd been able to turn the conversation over to Mrs. Keach. He thought of his meeting with Black, nodding every few moments as the woman droned on about life in Chicago and her late husband. When she stood to get dessert, he thanked her for supper and excused himself, making his way to his upstairs room.

His gun sat on the table where he left it. He felt naked without it, but the woman insisted no weapons were allowed at the table. Colt stripped out of his clothes, splashed water on his face, then stretched out on the bed. Resting his arms behind his head, he thought of Black Jolly.

As a U.S. Marshal, Colt had been given the task of locating the outlaw and bringing him back to Texas for trial. It had been a long search. Colt had followed the trail to Conviction, met with the sheriff, and learned of Black's actions against the MacLarens, including his subsequent retreat from the area.

While speaking with Brodie over breakfast, a young woman passed by their table, taking a seat with an older gentleman not far from them. Something about her appearance caught his attention. It wasn't the color of her hair or eyes that had him staring, but the way she tilted her head, her gestures. He couldn't put his finger on it, but he'd met her before, or someone much like her. The thought plagued him until he'd ridden north the following day, taking a chance Jolly might still be in the area. His hunch paid off.

Colt had been surprised Black didn't recognize him from the posse trailing him across Texas for several days. They'd been close several times. Close enough to look each other in the eyes. He doubted the outlaw knew his name, but thought he might recognize his face.

Of course, when Colt looked in the mirror, he sometimes didn't recognize himself, either. His clean-shaven face hid behind a week's worth of growth, and his dark hair had grown out until it almost touched his shoulders. Tonight, he'd held it in place with a strip of leather, something he would've laughed about a few months ago.

He'd entered the Lucky Lady for enough whiskey to wash down the trail dust. While leaning against the bar, his gaze had landed on Jolly. He'd almost choked on his drink. Biding his time, Colt struck up a conversation with the bartender, which led to him walking over to the outlaw's table. He could arrest him now and be done with it, but a part of him wanted to see what Jolly planned. Whatever it was, it would most certainly be against the law.

Highlander Ranch

"I don't recall ever having a venison roast as perfect as this one, Geneen." Caleb looked at what was left of the meat, debating whether to fork another piece onto his plate.

"I agree, lass. You'll have to be teaching me how to make it." Heather finished her last bite, pushing her plate away. "Although I'll never be as good a cook as you."

"All you need is practice."

Geneen glanced across the table at Nate. He'd yet to say a word about the meal or his day in town. In fact, he'd barely acknowledged her, his features showing none of the warmth and flirtation of the night before when his dark gaze had sent ripples of desire through her.

"What would you be thinking of the meal, Nate?"

He looked up at Heather's question, his gaze moving to Geneen. "It's very good."

Heather glanced at Geneen, then back at Nate. "Are you feeling all right, lad?"

"I'm fine." He absently rubbed his left arm, unaware how they all took notice. "If you don't mind, I'm going to head over to Archie's and bunk down early." Pushing from the table, he didn't bother to pick up his plate. Instead, he left the room and walked out the front door, not making eye contact with any of them.

"Maybe I should go see if he's all right." Geneen didn't wait for Caleb or Heather to comment before following him outside. "Nate." When he continued toward the foreman's house, she tried again. "Nate, wait."

Stopping, he turned around, his eyes distant and features menacing. "What is it, Geneen?"

116

His cold manner had her halting a few feet away, crossing her arms over her stomach. "I was worried about you. Are you certain you're feeling all right?"

Glaring at her, he nodded. "I told Heather I was, so yes, I'm fine."

His harsh words had her taking a faltering step away.

"Is there something else?" The hard tone of his voice had her flinching.

Her chest squeezed as she tightened her arms around her waist. "No. There's nothing else. I'm sorry to have bothered you." Turning, she hurried to the house, ignoring him when he called her name.

Nate hated watching her leave. He'd hurt her again without meaning to, but he had a sudden urge to get away, a persistent voice in his head pushing him to seek solace in the one thing that could destroy him.

He'd left the opium behind in Conviction and had no intention of ever using again. Unfortunately, his mind refused to accept the fact his body no longer needed the drug. Shaking his head in disgust, Nate continued on to the foreman's house. He needed whiskey and time alone.

The thought stopped him in his tracks. Both Doc Tilden and the doctor in San Francisco had told him when the urge arose not to seek relief in alcohol or be alone. They'd counseled him to spend time with family and friends, not allowing the desire to control him.

Shoving his right hand into a pocket, he lowered his head, letting out a deep breath. He fought the dueling messages in his brain. One told him to deaden his senses with whiskey, the other to turn around, go back inside and apologize. Neither appealed to him.

Deciding a third choice existed, Nate stalked to the corral beside the barn, whistling for Nomad. Ten minutes later, he headed out, unsure of his destination and not caring where he ended up.

Chapter Nine

Geneen couldn't sleep after hearing Nate ride off. Sitting by the window, wrapped up in a warm quilt, she'd stared outside, willing him to return. He didn't. Not that night or the next. When he didn't appear at breakfast the second morning in a row, she saddled Gypsy.

"Are you going to town, lass?"

Nodding, Geneen tightened the cinch around her horse's belly. "He may not want to see me, and that's fine. I just need to know he's all right before I leave."

Heather stepped next to her. "What are you saying?"

Geneen gripped the saddle horn with both hands, resting her forehead against the saddle. "I've decided to go back to Circle M for a while. Spend Christmas with the family."

"And get away from Nate."

Lifting her head, Geneen didn't try to hide the hurt she felt. "It's too hard seeing him struggle and not being able to help. I know I pushed him away, but I never gave up, not the way he has with me. I'm not strong enough to keep doing this with him."

Heather's brows furrowed. "Doing what, lass?"

"Pretending I don't care when I still love him as much as ever. How many times do you let a man ride away, allow him to break your heart?"

"I've no answer for you. It's a decision you'll need to be making for yourself. I do know we'll miss you being here. Won't you consider staying until after Christmas? Caleb and I will take a few days and go back with you. I know he won't be letting you ride back alone."

Geneen looked away, feeling guilty for what she had planned. "I thought to send a message to Brodie, asking if one of his deputies could accompany me back."

"Seems you've been thinking a lot on this."

Leaning against the stall, Geneen stared out the front of the barn, watching as two birds circled around each other above the house. They seemed so carefree and happy. She wanted to feel the same, yet didn't know how to get there.

"Since the hunt. He wanted to talk, but I pushed him away. I wasn't ready."

Heather rested a shoulder against the stall, watching her. "And now you are?"

"No. Not yet. That's why I want to go back to Circle M. I no longer know what I want." She turned to face Heather. "I hate leaving you and Caleb without more help."

Pushing away from the stall, Heather shook her head. "If you're set on going, send the telegram, but to Uncle Ewan, not Brodie. Ewan will send someone to get you without Brodie losing a deputy. Caleb and I will find someone to work for us while you're gone."

"What if I don't come back?"

"Then it will be because you've found your answer, lass, the same way I found mine about Caleb. No one can be doing it for you." Walking over to Gypsy, Heather picked up the reins, handing them to Geneen. "Now, off with you. The sooner you ride to town, the sooner you'll know what you'll be doing."

Kissing Heather's cheek, she mounted, reining Gypsy toward town. She'd dreaded the conversation with a woman she thought of as another sister. Now she felt a little better. Geneen had choices to make, and Heather wasn't going to try to dissuade her from them.

Riding toward Settlers Valley, she thought of Nate, wondering if he'd even agree to see her. There wasn't much she wanted to say, if anything. Once she determined he was all right, she'd send a telegram to Ewan and wait for his reply. She didn't see a reason to inform Nate. Caleb and Heather would tell him when he decided to return to the ranch. He might even decide to come back sooner once he learned she'd be leaving.

They'd both be free to do whatever they wanted and ignore the pain they'd caused each other. The thought gave her less comfort than she expected.

"Nate's in the back. Do you want me to get him?"

Geneen shook her head. "No, Mr. Kamm. I just wanted to know if he'd made it to town. He didn't seem himself the other night and hasn't returned to the ranch. Now that I know he's all right, I'll let him be."

"If you're sure."

"I am. Thank you." Gripping Gypsy's reins, she walked down the street, needing the time to compose the telegram to Ewan. Archie had told them about a different trail to Conviction and Circle M, one cutting the journey to less than five hours. She needed to remember to let the MacLarens know once she heard back from Ewan.

Decision made, she felt a spark of excitement at seeing her sister, Sarah, and the rest of the MacLarens. No matter what happened between her and Nate, she didn't plan to be gone too long. Caleb and Heather would need help getting the cattle ready to drive south, and she planned to be there.

Stepping into the telegraph office, she smiled at the man behind the counter.

"Yes, ma'am. What can I do for you?"

"I'd like to send a telegram to Conviction."

Grabbing a pencil and paper, he looked up. "What would you like to say?"

"Coming home. Need escort. Please advise. Geneen."

"And who is this going to?"

"Mr. Ewan MacLaren at Circle M Ranch."

The clerk looked up, his brows lifting. "Yes, ma'am. I'll get this right off."

After returning to the ranch, Geneen finished her chores, then began packing her few belongings. Ewan would respond soon. He didn't waste time when a family member requested help. The tug to return to Circle M had eased a little since sending the telegram, but not enough for her to change her mind.

Heather stepped into the bedroom, wiping her hands down her apron. "There's a lad downstairs with a telegram for you." She looked at the clothes laid out. "It appears you'll be leaving us soon."

"It all depends on what Ewan says." Walking past Heather into the hall, a strong pull of regret washed over her. Telling herself the absence would be temporary, she made her way down the stairs to the front door. "You have a telegram for me?"

A boy of about fourteen nodded. "Yes, ma'am. I was told it was important and to give it to you directly. I can wait for a reply." He handed her the message.

Reading through it, she bit her lip, holding back the emotion Ewan's quick response caused. "Please return a message that I'll be waiting at Highlander Ranch."

"Yes, ma'am."

Closing the door, she turned to Heather, her eyes brimming with tears. "He's sending Blaine and Fletcher for me. They'll be free to come within a few days."

Heather took the message from Geneen's outstretched hand and read it. "Uncle Ewan didn't waste time. So why are you crying?"

Swiping at the moisture on her cheeks, she shook her head. "It's silly."

Heather turned toward the kitchen. "Well, you can tell me why it would be silly while we fix supper. We've enough fresh venison for steaks, and I'll be fixing cabbage."

"I'll prepare the potatoes and biscuits." Slipping on an apron, Geneen grabbed several potatoes and set a pot of water on the stove.

"And we've vinegar pie from last night." Heather glanced at her friend, letting out a slow breath. "You don't need to be going, you know."

Geneen stopped what she was doing to look at Heather. "It's best I do, at least for a while. Whatever Nate and I had is gone. Wishing it was still the same only makes it worse." Cleaning the potatoes, she cut them into cubes, adding them to the pot. "I do mean to return."

"Seeing Sarah and the rest of the family will be good for you, lass."

Geneen nodded. "Don't you miss them, Heather?"

"Aye, but my life is here with Caleb now. We've our own ranch and dreams." Wiping her hands down the apron, she looked out the window at the hills in the distance. "We've so many plans, including having bairns."

Swallowing the pain at her own desire for the same, Geneen mixed the biscuits, then checked the amount of wood in the stove. She loved working the ranch, helping with all the chores needed to raise cattle.

Riding was a passion, something she could do for hours and never tire. Her skills with a gun were exemplary, and she seldom flinched under pressure. And although she loved to cook and help the women, she'd seldom thought of falling in love and marriage. When she'd met Nate, her outlook on life changed.

Since that first day, Geneen believed they were meant to be together. Falling in love had been effortless. When the pain Nate thought he had under control worsened, he began to shut her out, spending little time at the ranch when he wasn't on duty as a deputy.

The MacLaren family stepped in, doing their best to help. It wasn't enough. When Nate left, her heart broke. She clung to the hope he'd return. After a few months passed without any word, Geneen began to give up.

Caleb's marriage to Heather, and his decision to buy the ranch from Archie, had been her chance to move past the pain and start fresh. Their enthusiasm made her decision to stay in Settlers Valley easy. Then Nate showed himself.

His appearance had been a blessing and a curse. Geneen felt relief, knowing he was safe. The fact he'd been living less than a day's ride away broke her heart a second time. He'd been close, wanting nothing to do with her, except perhaps to explain his reasons for leaving.

Giving up her first love, allowing herself a chance with someone else, hadn't been her plan. Geneen now saw it as a way to get past the hurt and allow Nate to do the same.

Nate forced himself to stay in town, living in the cramped shack behind the livery. He'd made a mess of mending his past mistakes with Geneen, and returning to the ranch in his current state wouldn't help. Staying away seemed best until he could find a way to fix the hurt he'd caused.

After a week living at the ranch, isolating himself hadn't been easy. Marcus instinctively knew work would be Nate's salvation, piling as much on him as possible. He'd made a third and final dredge for Nettles, surprised the man never mentioned Nate's part in letting the Indian boy get away. The orders for more work kept coming, forcing him to start before sunup and work until his body was too tired to do any more.

For the first time in weeks, his head began to clear. The desire for opium lessened each day until he woke one morning and didn't think of it until almost noon. Still, he decided to stay in town a few more days, make certain the vile substance had no hold on him before approaching Geneen. He couldn't afford to make one more mistake.

"There are a couple men asking for you."

Nate set down the hammer, straightening on a groan as he turned toward Marcus.

"Did they say their names?"

"MacLaren is all I heard."

Wiping his arm across his brow, Nate picked up the shirt he'd removed and slipped into it. "Thanks."

Moving past Marcus, he walked into the front of the livery, a slow smile crossing his face when he saw Blaine and Fletcher.

"Nate. It's good to see you." Blaine extended his hand, followed by Fletcher.

Grasping one, then the other, Nate looked them over, his grin still in place. "Appears you've been on the trail a while."

Blaine nodded. "Aye, we have. We've come to fetch Geneen."

Nate stared at him, not sure he'd heard him right. "Geneen?"

"Aye. She sent a telegram to Da, asking if he could send someone to escort her home." Fletcher glanced at his cousin. "I volunteered, as did Blaine."

He blinked, their meaning still not registering. "Geneen sent a telegram to your father?"

Fletcher nodded, then glanced at Blaine again, their expressions confused. "Aye, lad. Da received the message a few days ago. The lass didn't tell you?"

Shoulders sagging, Nate shook his head. "I haven't stayed at Caleb's in several nights. We, um, well...Geneen and I didn't part well before I rode back to town."

Blaine's gaze narrowed on him. "You've a habit of not parting well with the lass, Nate."

Gut clenching, a muscle in his jaw ticked as he thought of the mess he'd created with Geneen. Pacing several steps away, he shredded his hand through his hair, wondering how he could change her mind.

Then it occurred to him—this might be what she truly wanted, what might be best for both of them. She'd finally given up, deciding he wasn't worth her love. As much as he wanted to, Nate couldn't argue with the logic. Taking several deep breaths, he turned around.

"It's a good decision." Nodding at them, he walked toward the back door.

"That's all you've to say, lad?" Blaine's eyes held a fiery glare.

Stopping, Nate lowered his head. Closing his eyes, he tried to calm the piercing pain in his chest before glancing over his shoulder.

"What more is there to say? Geneen's a grown woman and makes her own decisions. If going back to Circle M is what she wants, so be it."

"Wait," Fletcher called out before Nate left. "Come to supper tonight. Talk to the lass. It may be the last time you'll see her for quite a while."

Nate pushed aside the ball of fire lodged in his stomach. "When do you head home?"

Blaine took a step toward him. "Tomorrow. We've no time to stay longer."

His face a mask once more, Nate turned and shook their hands. "Have a safe trip."

Highlander Ranch

"Nate said nothing else. Only that he thought Geneen had made a good decision." Blaine cast an apologetic glance at her, seeing pain flash in her eyes. "I'm sorry if that's not what you wanted to hear, lass."

Throat clogged with emotion, she shook her head, willing away the tears. "It's not your fault, Blaine. Nate made the decision to leave me behind a long time ago." Sucking in a shaky breath, she forced a smile. "It's truly time I return to Circle M." She looked at Heather and Caleb. "But I'll be back before spring roundup."

Sitting next to her, Blaine placed a hand on her arm. "Are you certain this is what you want, lass?"

The way everyone looked at her, Geneen knew they doubted she'd made the right decision. And although her heart ached, she still believed returning to Circle M would help her deal with

Nate's rejection easier than if she stayed in Settlers Valley.

She straightened her shoulders, lifting her chin. "Yes, I am. Now, tell us what's happening at Circle M."

Chapter Ten

Caleb waited until Saturday night. When Nate still failed to return to the ranch a couple days after Geneen left, he'd ridden into town. He found his friend in the Lucky Lady, a full glass of whiskey in front of him.

"You want company?" Caleb nodded to the chair across from Nate.

"Suit yourself." He held up his hand, signaling for another whiskey.

"You been staring at your drink for a while?"

Nate looked at Caleb, seeing the glint in his friend's eyes. He couldn't help a wry grin from spreading across his face. "Close to an hour."

They sat in silence for a while, listening to the tinny sound of the new piano delivered by steamship that week. A group of miners walked in, taking a table not far away. Ordering drinks, they talked in low voices, paying no attention to those around them.

The miners had been in the saloon about twenty minutes when Sheriff Polk walked in, heading straight for their table. Refusing the chair they offered, he leaned down, talking to them in a voice too quiet to hear what was said.

At one point, Polk's face reddened, his voice rising before he caught himself. Several more minutes passed before he straightened and looked around the saloon. His gaze stilled on Nate and Caleb for an instant before he turned, walking out.

"What do you think that was about?"

Nate shook his head. "No idea. If Polk's involved, it can't be good."

Picking up his whiskey, Caleb took a slow sip. "What do you know about the man?"

"Polk?"

Caleb nodded.

"Not much more than what Marcus has told me. It's clear to most townsfolk the sheriff is paid by Nettles to look the other way when needed. He does help guard the gold once it reaches town."

"Have they ever had any trouble with shipments?"

"Not that I've heard." Nate watched a man he'd never seen before walk into the saloon, taking a spot at the bar. Picking up the drink the bartender handed him, he turned, resting against the bar as he scanned the room. When his gaze landed on Nate, he nodded, then shifted around to face the bartender. "Marcus says he brings the gold to town in small amounts, delivering it to the bank. The sheriff assembles guards, paid by Nettles, to watch it until the steamship arrives, or until transport by wagon to Conviction can be arranged. Eventually, the gold ends up in San Francisco."

Nate kept his attention on the man at the bar. Something about him seemed familiar, but he couldn't place him. "Do you know the man at the bar in the long overcoat and brown hat?"

Caleb glanced over and shook his head. "Never seen him. Why?"

Nate continued to study the man. "He came by the livery this week to have his horse checked. Marcus fixed a couple horseshoes, got paid, and the man left. Something about him seems familiar." Shaking his head, Nate took another sip of whiskey.

"So Polk hires the guards, but they're not deputies." Caleb stole another quick look around the saloon.

"Nope. Men he hires."

Caleb rolled his glass between his fingers. "Nettles's private army."

Nate considered Caleb's words, his brows furrowing. "I suppose you could say that. Personally, I think Polk does whatever Nettles orders him to do. Hiring guards to watch the gold while it's being held at the bank is one of his jobs, and from what Marcus says, he gets paid well to do it. Is it illegal? Probably not. A conflict of interest? It could be if he puts his work for Nettles before what he's paid to do for the town."

Tossing back the last of the whiskey, Caleb set his glass down. "Settlers Valley needs someone like Brodie...or you." Standing, he ignored Nate's look of surprise. "Tomorrow's Sunday. Heather expects you home for supper. With Geneen gone, there's no reason for you to stay away." Shoving his chair back in place, Caleb sent him a stern glare. "Be there."

Circle M Ranch

"Kyla invited a couple extra people for Sunday supper." Sarah continued to set out plates for the weekly family supper. This Sunday, it would be at Kyla's, where Colin and Sarah lived with their young son, Grant. Geneen and Kyla had a close bond, and she couldn't love Colin's mother more if she were her own.

"Did Kyla say who she invited?" Geneen set coffee cups around the table, counting to make certain she'd brought out enough.

"Brodie gave two of his deputies the day off, telling them it had been too long since they'd been to the ranch. You remember Seth and Alex, don't you?"

Geneen did. One stood tall and lean with dark hair and eyes, and a brooding nature. The other had fair skin, blue eyes, and a steady gaze that had bored into her the first time they met. She'd remembered thinking either would be intimidating to anyone on the wrong side of the law.

"Of course. I believe Brodie hired them after Nate left town."

Sarah nodded. "He did. Says they're both real good." She looked up when Colin walked in with Grant on his shoulders.

"Mama." Grant reached his arms out, giggling when she took him from Colin.

"The table looks grand, lasses. What are Ma and the aunts fixing?" He glanced toward the kitchen.

Sarah rested Grant on her hip. "Beef and venison."

Geneen's heart caught, remembering their hunt less than two weeks before. She'd been back at Circle M for a couple days, setting into a routine as if she'd never left. Enough time had passed she'd almost forgotten the size of the ranch, the way everyone hustled about, doing their chores without being told.

She'd yet to saddle Gypsy to ride out with them. They didn't need her the same as Caleb and Heather. The thought had plagued her since returning, the guilt building a little every day until she found it hard to reconcile the reason she'd felt compelled to leave.

Nate. She'd left because of him.

It seemed such a weak excuse for leaving her friends without help. Geneen hadn't told anyone, including Sarah, but she already planned to go back well before Caleb and Heather rounded up the herd for the drive south. Maybe as soon as a couple weeks after Christmas.

If the weather held, she'd go by herself. The trail Archie knew about cut the ride down to about five hours, an easy trip if she left at sunrise. They hadn't come across anyone on the trail. It had been quick and uneventful.

"Did you hear me, Geneen?"

She blinked at Sarah's voice. "I'm sorry. What did you say?"

"Would you mind watching Grant for a bit? Colin wants to show me something in the barn."

"Not at all." Taking Grant from her arms, Geneen followed Sarah out onto the front porch. Watching her sister and Colin walk away, her chest squeezed when he took his wife's hand, smiling over at her.

Geneen had never felt a twinge of jealousy at her sister's strong relationship with Colin. They'd been lucky to find each other after years of separation, and deserved to be happy. Nevertheless, she couldn't stop the tightening of her throat or ache in her heart.

Grant squirmed in her arms, twisting to look at two men riding up. Geneen hadn't even noticed Seth and Alex approaching. Waving, she took the steps down to the yard, forcing a smile as the men reined to a stop and dismounted.

Both removed their hats, but it was Alex who walked closer, his gaze wandering over her. "Good afternoon, Miss MacGregor. Brodie told us you returned to the ranch."

She felt her face heat at what appeared to be interest in his gaze. Alex had never met Nate, probably knew nothing of her history with Brodie's former deputy, and wouldn't know her reason for returning to Circle M.

"I arrived a couple days ago."

He reached out, letting Grant's tiny hand grasp a finger. "I'm sure it's good to be home."

She watched as he played easily with the boy. A rugged lawman, a pair of guns strapped around his waist, comfortable showing an interest in a small child.

"It is. I missed everyone, although I miss Caleb and Heather. There's so much to do at their ranch." She blew out a breath, shifting Grant to her hip.

"May I?" Alex reached out his hands, taking the squirming boy from her.

Laughing when her nephew placed his chubby hands on Alex's cheeks and squeezed, she felt the earlier awkwardness begin to ease. For the first time in weeks, she felt herself relax.

Highlander Ranch

"It's good you've come back to the ranch, lad. Staying behind the livery isn't right when we've plenty of room here." Heather set down her fork, then stood. "I'll bring out dessert."

After the kitchen door closed behind her, Nate looked at Caleb. "You didn't need to move my belongings here. I'm fine staying with Archie."

He arrived a little after noon to find his clothes moved to an upstairs guest room in the main house. Nate hadn't been to the second floor before today, surprised at how large the inside seemed compared to how it looked from the outside. Caleb had mentioned Archie telling him about his late wife and how they'd wanted a houseful of children. After her death, he'd never remarried, living alone in a house built to accommodate a large family never meant to be.

"Heather did it yesterday when I rode into town to find you. I'm glad she did. Archie prefers to eat alone in the foreman's house. After living with all the MacLarens, and with Geneen gone, it seems too quiet in this place with just me and Heather."

Nate didn't respond right away. He'd been doing his best to keep his thoughts off Geneen returning to Circle M and a family that meant a great deal to her. He opened his mouth to reply, stopping at the sound of a loud knock on the front door.

"Are you expecting someone?"

Caleb shook his head, standing. "Nope."

He walked to the entry, picking up his shotgun before opening the door. His body stilled, features going blank. Walking up behind him, a gun in his right hand, Nate studied the stranger standing on the porch. His leather pants and shirt looked to be made of deerskin, his hat an intricate basket weave with tiny beads for decoration.

"Are you the owner?"

Caleb stepped forward. "I am."

The stranger extended his hand, ignoring the shotgun. "Jedidiah Coates."

"Caleb Stewart, Mr. Coates." He grasped his hand, nodding behind him. "This is Nate Hollis."

"Friends call me Jed." He held out his hand to Nate.

Holstering his gun, Nate shook Jed's hand, his gaze landing on three Indians standing behind him. "And those men?"

Stepping aside, he gestured to the three dark-skinned men. "They're the reason I'm here. These three are Maidu headsmen. The one on the far left has a son. He believes you helped him and came to offer his thanks."

The one he mentioned came forward, holding a large intricately woven basket. Extending his hands toward Caleb, the man dipped his head slightly, muttering something neither Caleb nor Nate understood.

"He's offering the basket as his way of thanking you for saving his son's life," Jed explained, looking at Caleb. "This one is for you."

Another of the Indians took a step forward, holding out a second basket.

"This one is for Nate."

When neither moved to accept the baskets, Jed lowered his voice. "It would dishonor them if you don't accept their gifts."

"What is this?" Heather moved between Caleb and Nate, her gaze moving to the men outside. "I'm Heather Stewart, Caleb's wife."

"Jed Coates, ma'am. These three are Maidu headsmen from the village a few miles north of here."

Caleb placed a hand on the small of Heather's back. "The man to the left is the Indian boy's father. He came to thank us for helping his son escape."

She looked at the others. "Ach. There's no need to be thanking us. We did what was right."

Clearing his throat, Caleb nodded at the baskets. "He brought the baskets to thank us. Jed says it would be an insult not to accept them."

Her eyes widened in understanding. "Then you must be coming inside. You can be joining us for dessert."

Jed shook his head. "We don't want to intrude, ma'am."

"You won't be. And my name's Heather." Turning around, she went back into the kitchen.

Caleb chuckled. "Don't consider arguing with her, Jed. It would be a waste of time. Come on in and have a seat."

Jed turned to the three Maidu, speaking to them in their language. Hesitating a moment, the three spoke among themselves, one man's voice a little louder and more commanding than the other two. He looked at Jed and nodded.

The three moved past Jed, Caleb, and Nate, following the path Heather took to the kitchen. Standing together, they looked around, their gazes taking in the furniture, pictures, and dishes on the table.

"Please, sit down." Heather held a pie in one hand, more plates in the other. She set them next to the ones already on the table. Pulling out a chair, she nodded to the seat before sitting, demonstrating what she asked.

The Indian boy's father moved first, taking a seat, his back straight. The other two followed.

Within a few minutes, everyone had a piece of pie before them, the Indians not sure what to do. After Caleb picked up his fork and took a bite, Nate and Jed followed. A moment later, the three Maidu headsmen did the same, fumbling with the unfamiliar utensils. One at a time, they grew accustomed to them, their pie disappearing in small bites.

"How did you come to be with them, Jed?" Nate sat back, watching as the man finished his pie and set down his fork.

"My wife is Maidu. I was out on a hunt when the incident with the boy happened or we would've been here sooner."

Nate nodded. "We wondered where the boy went. He took off while we talked to the men from the mine."

Jed's features hardened. "I won't tell you your business, but some of those miners are plain mean. Leland Nettles orders his men to shoot any Indians who come near the camp." He couldn't conceal the disgust in his voice. "The Maidu are a peaceful tribe. They don't farm and don't own horses. They hunt and gather what they need to live. They do tend to a small grove of oak trees near the village."

"For the acorns?" Nate asked.

Jed nodded. "It's one of their main sources of food."

"You live in the village with your wife?"

Shaking his head at Heather, he picked up his cup of coffee, taking a sip. "We have our own place a mile or so away from the village. There are a number of Maidu villages spread out among the hills and valleys. Our ranch is between them."

Caleb's brow rose. "You're a rancher?"

"A few head of cattle and three horses. We also raise pigs, chickens, and have two milk cows. Not much, but it keeps us fed, and we sometimes supply meat to their village." He nodded at the three headsmen, who still worked on their pie. "Like I said, they don't farm, but they're excellent hunters when the miners don't interfere."

Nate finished his coffee, setting down the cup. "What happened that caused the miners to come after the boy?"

"He stumbled on the body of a man. A group of miners saw him and he ran. Kept running until he got to the lake and saw you. Over the years, whites have driven the Maidu farther into the hills and deeper into the valleys."

"Because of gold?" Caleb asked.

Jed nodded. "Mostly. The Maidu are easy targets because they don't put up much of a fight. They don't know how to. After generations of living peacefully, they found themselves hunted for no apparent reason, other than they're Indian. Leland Nettles is a nasty sort, as are the men who work for him. Sheriff Polk isn't any better, but you've most likely figured that out. The Maidu trust few whites. You are now counted in that number."

He looked down the table at the three Indians, saying something in their language. Looking back at Caleb, he pushed from the table. "We'll be leaving now." He glanced at Heather. "That was mighty fine pie, ma'am. Thank you."

"You're welcome here anytime, as are these other men." Heather rose from the table, smiling at the men. "I'll say goodbye to you."

They watched as she picked up plates, heading into the kitchen, before they walked through the house to the entry.

When they reached the front door, Jed stopped. "Be real careful of those miners and anyone associated with Nettles or Polk. Neither are up to any good." Stepping onto the porch, he looked between Nate and Caleb. "If you're ever up our way again, my ranch is about four miles northeast of the mine, up the Feather River."

"Wait. How are you getting back?" Nate asked.

"I'm on my horse. The others will walk to their village. They'll camp overnight, if needed." He shrugged. "It's their way."

Nodding at the Maidu headsmen as they left, Caleb closed the door. "Jed has no love for Nettles."

"Or for Polk. I can't say as I blame him."

"I'm serious about it being time to replace Polk."

Nate's jaw worked as he thought about the sheriff. "If you're thinking of me replacing him, I'm not sure that's a good idea. I'm not the man I was while in Conviction."

Caleb crossed his arms. "The hell you aren't. I've been watching. I don't see a trace of the man who came to Circle M, his body and mind controlled by opium. You're back to being the same man as when you first arrived in Conviction on the steamship. Heather sees it, and so did Geneen before you pushed her away...again. You're the only one who hasn't figured it out."

Lowering himself onto the sofa, Nate shredded his hand through his hair. "I made a mess of things with Geneen."

"Yes, you did. Don't continue to make a mess of your life."

Chapter Eleven

Colt sat at a table in the Lucky Lady Tuesday evening, watching and listening. He'd expected to hear from Black by now, but hadn't seen a trace of the man since meeting him the week before. And he'd heard nothing of gold being moved from the mine to town.

Keeping his gaze focused on the door, Colt lifted his glass of whiskey, taking a sip as a man with a partial left arm walked inside. Nate Hollis. He remembered him as a lawman in Texas, seeing him again Saturday night in deep conversation with another man. Colt knew Nate didn't recognize him, but neither had Black Jolly.

He watched as Nate headed to the bar and ordered a drink. His focus on him broke when Black entered the saloon.

As with any place Black frequented, conversation stopped and heads turned. He paid no attention. Instead, he cut a path straight toward Colt. Pulling out a chair, he sat down, leaning forward to rest his arms on the table.

"Thought I'd find you here."

Colt glanced over Black's shoulder long enough to see Nate turn around, his attention now on them.

"Do you have news for me?"

Black nodded. "Schedule's changed. I got news the mine is making smaller shipments over the next ten days instead of a larger one late this week."

Colt's hard expression didn't change. "Three times the work. Hope you negotiated more money."

Black glared at him. "Don't worry. You'll be taken care of."

Colt snorted. "I've heard that before."

"Don't push me, Dye. If I say you'll be taken care of, you will."

Colt let that settle a moment before appearing to accept it. "When?"

Lowering his voice, Black leaned farther across the table. "The first one is tomorrow. Be at the Acorn at nine in the morning. I'll already be there."

"How many other guards do you have?"

Pushing his chair from the table, Black stood. "Three, including me. Make sure your gun is loaded."

Colt watched him walk out, still surprised but glad the outlaw didn't recognize him from the posse. Sitting back, he let out a relieved breath.

"Mind if I join you?"

Jerking his gaze up, his eyes landed on Nate. Colt motioned to a chair.

Grabbing the back of it, he extended his hand. "I'm Nate Hollis."

Accepting it, Colt nodded. "I remember you from Nacogdoches."

Nate's grip tightened an instant before he let go of Colt's hand. "I don't recognize you."

"Colt Dye."

Nate's eyes widened. "The U.S. Marshal?" Sitting down, he looked at Colt's long hair tied at the nape of his head, several days' old stubble, and rumpled clothing. "What are you doing this far west?"

"Following the trail of an outlaw."

"The man who just left?"

Colt nodded. "Do you know him?"

"No. I've heard he's working for Leland Nettles, though. That information makes me not want to trust the man. What's his name and why do you want him?"

"Black Jolly. He's wanted for killings in Texas and a town south of here. Conviction."

Nate sat up, his casual manner disappearing. "Conviction?"

"You've been there?"

"Up until a few months ago, I worked as a deputy for Brodie MacLaren. I, uh...had some difficulties and had to get away."

"Then I'm guessing you haven't heard about the trouble at the Circle M."

Swallowing the uncomfortable knot in his throat, Nate shook his head. "Tell me."

As Colt explained about the attacks on the MacLaren ranch, Nate's stomach tightened, his chest restricting to a painful throbbing. Geneen, Caleb, and Heather had been there through it all, and not once had any of them mentioned the shootings, poisoned cattle, or threats. All their concern had been directed toward him. He'd never considered what they may have gone through after he left Conviction.

"Black is known for these types of attacks. I was ordered to find him not long after we arrested and hung those cattle thieves in Nacogdoches."

Scrubbing his hand down his face, Nate nodded. "They did more than rustle cattle."

"And deserved worse than a simple hanging. Sometimes the law's justice isn't enough."

"You're still a marshal, Colt. So it must be enough most of the time."

Shrugging, he motioned for a bottle and another glass. When the saloon girl walked over, she set them on the table, then left the men alone.

"Are you a deputy in Settlers Valley?" Colt reached for the bottle, pouring a drink for Nate and another for himself.

Nate shook his head. "I work for the blacksmith."

Colt chuckled as he sipped his whiskey. "A blacksmith, huh? From what I've heard around town, you'd be a better choice for a lawman than who they have now. No one seems too happy with Sheriff Polk."

Nate tossed back his whiskey, shaking his head in frustration. "My friends, Caleb and Heather Stewart, have said the same. They moved here a few months ago from Conviction."

"That must have been the man I saw you with Saturday night."

Nate nodded. "It is. Heather is a MacLaren...Brodie's cousin. I noticed you at the bar, but couldn't place where I'd seen you before. The long hair and short beard threw me."

"Apparently, Black hasn't placed me with the posse chasing him in Texas, which is good. He's hired me and another man to guard gold being moved from the mine to town."

"The gold won't make it."

Colt sipped his whiskey, nodding. "I agree. That's the reason I agreed to be a guard."

"To catch him in the act. Arrest him for that, then inform him of the other charges." Nate rubbed his chin. "You know, Black may decide to end it rather than be taken to jail."

A feral gleam brightened Colt's eyes. "I'm hoping he does. Hauling him back to Texas for a murder trial doesn't put me at ease."

"What about taking him to Conviction for the charges there? Didn't you say at least one man died?"

"Yeah. A MacLaren ranch hand." Colt sat back in his chair, considering the possibility. "I'll send a telegram to Brodie, find out what evidence he has and if it will stick. If it isn't enough, I don't want to risk the man getting off."

"He'd still face the charges in Texas."

Colt nodded. "True, and they've got solid witnesses to the killing of a local rancher."

The old rush of putting an outlaw behind bars pumped through Nate. He hadn't realized how much he missed being a lawman, bringing men to justice, keeping people safe.

"When's the first shipment?"

Colt's gaze narrowed a little. "Nine tomorrow morning. I meet Black and the other men he hired at the mine."

"Nettles staggers the shipments, but seems to take the same route each trip. I'll be waiting a couple miles north of town. There's a rock outcropping along the river with good cover."

"You don't have to do that, Nate."

Pinching the bridge of his nose, Nate glanced up. "There hasn't been a lot I've had to do the last few months, other than stay alive. Watching out for you is something I have to do."

Colt's brow rose, an amused grin tilting up the corners of his mouth. "What about protecting the gold?"

Barking out a laugh, Nate rested an arm on the table. "I don't give a damn about the gold or its owner. They can both fall to the bottom of Feather River for all I care. What I do care about is helping you bring an outlaw to justice. Maybe doing something good will help me put my other transgressions in a better light."

Colt studied him. Nate didn't seem to be a man troubled by past misdeeds, someone who needed to get away from a good life in a town with people who seemed to care about him. It made Colt wonder what had happened to cause a good lawman to forsake the badge to work in a livery. It was a question that wouldn't be answered today.

Tilting his glass toward Nate, he nodded. "So be it. I'm glad to have you along."

Circle M

Christmas loomed less than ten days away, but Geneen couldn't feel any enthusiasm for the holiday. Each day, she found herself thinking of Nate more, not less, wondering if she'd made a huge mistake leaving Settlers Valley. Sarah loved

153

having her back, telling Geneen to give it a little more time before deciding whether to return to Highlander Ranch.

In a short time, Caleb's ranch had become her home, a place she felt needed and appreciated to a greater degree than at Circle M. As the largest ranch north of Sacramento, the MacLarens had their pick of ranch hands, fostered solid relationships with cattle buyers, and included a family who'd grown up raising cattle and horses. Caleb and Heather still had a great deal of building to do, which excited Geneen. She wanted to be a part of their success.

"I wondered where you disappeared to after supper." Sarah sat next to Geneen on the porch swing, setting an almost completed quilt on her lap. They rocked back and forth, saying nothing for several minutes as they stared out over the distant mountains. "Christmas is almost here."

Geneen nodded, not taking her gaze from the star-filled heavens. The temperatures had dropped a little each night since her return. Not enough for snow, but cold enough for everyone to bundle up in heavy coats when outside.

"Are you planning to stay?"

A grim smile crossed Geneen's face at her sister's question. "You asked me the same question yesterday. And the day before."

Folding her hands together on top of the quilt, Sarah glanced at Geneen. "You've been so quiet. It's beginning to worry me. Kyla and Colin are concerned about you, too. Is it being away from Caleb and Heather that bothers you so much, or what happened with Nate?"

"I've been wondering the same. Being here has given me time to think about why I left. The conclusion I've come to is it's a mixture of reasons. I do miss Heather and Caleb. We became close the last few months and work well together." She looked at Sarah. "We've a routine that worked for us. I know they have a great deal more work with me gone."

"Maybe we should ask Ewan about sending help. Maybe Blaine or Fletch."

Geneen shook her head. "It wouldn't be right to take them away from their duties here."

Sarah twisted her hands in the quilt, biting her lower lip, thinking about what she'd heard around the ranch. "I've heard some rumors."

Shifting in the swing, Geneen tugged at her coat, huddling deep inside its warmth. "Rumors?"

"Uncle Ewan and Uncle Ian are considering making changes. If they do, the decision will affect everyone."

Geneen leaned toward her. "What have you heard?"

Sarah looked around, then behind her, making certain no one could hear them. "You know Sean has been desperate to go to veterinary school," she whispered, mentioning Ian's oldest son.

Geneen nodded. "He wants to attend Highland Society's Veterinary School in Edinburgh, Sarah. He'd be gone for years, living in Scotland...alone."

"It's true. Colin, Quinn, and Brodie have been encouraging the uncles to consider it. He's so smart and gifted."

Looking back out at the mountains, she thought of Sean being gone. His skills saved many animals on the ranch. He kept abreast of the latest therapies and cures, reading everything he could order from back east and Europe.

"Does the family have the money to send him?"

Sarah nodded. "Colin says they would make do. Blaine and Fletch are very good with the animals."

"Not as skilled as Sean."

"No. But his heart is set on going. Several of us are afraid he'll take off one day to fulfill his dream, with or without the family's blessing."

Blowing out a breath, Geneen nodded. "When would he go?"

"If the uncles decide to send him, he'd leave within a few months."

"He's so sweet and quiet, Sarah. I don't know if I've ever heard him raise his voice."

"His quiet is deceptive. He doesn't hesitate to speak his mind or protect the ranch the same as everyone else. He just has a different way about him."

Geneen grinned. "He's a peacemaker."

"He is. The uncles are going to decide by Christmas, maybe sooner." Sarah waited a moment before surprising her with one more possible change. "Blaine and Colin aren't getting along."

Geneen's jaw dropped. "I've been here a week and seen nothing."

"They seldom work together anymore. Haven't you noticed Blaine living with Uncle Ian and Aunt Gail? Colin and Blaine got into a major fight several weeks ago. No one could get between them without getting hit themselves. It was a blessing neither broke any bones. The cuts and bruises were enough. We hauled them into town in the wagon so Doc Tilden could stitch them up." Sarah gripped the quilt tighter, a shudder rippling through her. "It was awful, Geneen. When they got home, Blaine packed his things and moved to Ian's. They've spoken no more than four or five words since."

Geneen felt as if a bolt of lightning had speared her. "They've always been so close. Colin the oldest son and Blaine the second oldest."

"It seems Blaine is tired of Colin ordering him around, trying to take their father's place instead of being the older brother." Sarah shook her head on a long sigh. "They haven't worked together since we came back from Heather's wedding."

"What are the uncles thinking of doing?"

Sarah glanced behind them at the sound of someone coughing inside, waiting to make certain they didn't step out onto the porch.

"As far as I know, the uncles haven't spoken of the rift to anyone. Whatever they may be considering, I believe it involves Blaine."

Chapter Twelve

Settlers Valley

"The trip couldn't have been easier. We didn't see anyone, and Black never made a move to take over the wagon. The sheriff met us at the bank with his men, we unloaded, and Black took off." Colt leaned against a post at the livery.

Setting down the bridle he'd been working on, Nate straightened. "I followed the wagon the last quarter mile. When I didn't see anyone and Black didn't make a move, I turned off at the edge of town."

Colt scrubbed a hand down his face. "Maybe I'm wrong and he's in it for whatever money Nettles is paying him. The gold might not be a factor."

"So arrest Black and haul him back to Conviction."

Shaking his head, Colt rubbed the back of his neck. "I can't shake the feeling he's after a load and is waiting for the right moment. The man doesn't know how to live unless he's robbing or hurting someone."

Crossing his arms, Nate looked through the open doorway to the forge. Marcus worked on a set of horseshoes, paying no attention to the men in back. "When's the next shipment?"

"I don't know. Black rode off right after we unloaded the gold. My guess is I'll hear from him the night before the next load, the same as before."

"Let me know."

Colt shook his head. "There's no reason for you to be involved, Nate."

"If Black's plan is to take the gold, he'll kill you and the other guard. He isn't going to share the wealth with anyone."

"I'll be ready if that's what he intends."

"You can't be vigilant all the time, Colt." Nate picked up the bridle, holding it up to check his work. "All you need to do is tell me when Black needs you at the mine."

"Assuming he plans to guard another shipment."

Chuckling, Nate stared up at him. "Do you truly believe Black set himself up in this position without intending to steal whatever he can?"

Colt pursed his lips, shaking his head. "No. There's a reason for every move the man makes."

"The way I see it, you have two choices. Arrest him and haul him back to Conviction...maybe on to Texas. Or stay with him until he makes a move. If he does what you think, you can arrest him to stand trial in Settlers Valley." Nate tugged on the bridle, making certain the work he'd done would hold, then set it down. "Of course, if his intent is to steal the gold, the man could end up getting himself shot."

Colt didn't try to suppress a slight grin. "It's been known to happen."

"Colt?" Marcus walked toward them, holding out a piece of paper. "This is for you."

"Thanks." Taking it, he read the contents of the short telegram, not looking up as he read it aloud. "'Bring to Conviction. Giles Delacroix to testify against Jolly.'" He glanced at Nate. "It's from Brodie. Do you want to hear what else he wrote?"

Nodding, he swiped an arm across his forehead. "Sure."

"'Bring Nate back with you.'" Chuckling, Colt folded the message, sliding it into a pocket. "Your lady is in Conviction and your old job is waiting. What's keeping you here?"

"Hey now. Don't be trying to lose me the best man I've had since coming to Settlers Valley," Marcus grumbled before turning around to return to the forge.

Nate watched his boss walk away, feeling a stab of guilt at the thought of leaving. Looking at Colt, he saw the question in the man's eyes.

"Marcus has been good to me."

Colt continued to stare at him. "No one's said otherwise."

"He'd be in a bind if I left."

Nodding, Colt shifted enough to see Marcus working at the forge. "True."

Nate's face tightened. "Geneen left on her own. She may not want me following after her."

"Maybe not." Colt turned to leave, then glanced over his shoulder at Nate. "There's one way to find out."

Nate snorted, but kept his mouth shut.

"It's a short ride. Guess you'll know when you're ready, Hollis."

Nate didn't reply as Colt walked out a side gate toward the street. He'd been plagued with thoughts of Geneen for months, ever since leaving the Circle M. When she'd shown up in Settlers Valley, he thought they might still have a chance. Her determination to push him away, not listen to his reasons for leaving, raised more doubt than hope.

The night she'd tried to talk, he'd been struggling with his continuing desire for opium. Nate pushed her away, unable to talk about something he didn't understand himself. He'd spent the night in the old shack behind the livery, waking the next morning with a sense of clarity he hadn't had in almost a year.

Nate didn't know what prompted the change and didn't care. He'd sat up on the old cot, scrubbed his hand down his face, and knew he could overcome anything if he had Geneen in his life.

What he should've done was ride back to Highlander Ranch, do whatever it took to get her to talk to him. Instead, he'd waited a day, then another, making certain what he felt that first morning stuck. He took too long.

By then, Blaine and Fletcher had come to escort her home. He hadn't voiced his thoughts to Caleb or Heather, but in his heart, Nate hadn't given up. There were things he needed to do in Settlers Valley, decisions he needed to make. And he refused to leave before Colt discovered what Black Jolly had planned.

Colt sat at the supper table at the boardinghouse, sipping coffee, barely hearing the conversation between the two other boarders as he pondered what to do next. It had been several days and two more shipments since the first wagonload he'd guarded. Both times, they made it to town without a hint of trouble.

"Wasn't that you guarding the ore shipment this morning, Mr. Dye?"

It took him a moment to realize Mrs. Keach spoke to him. Setting down his cup, he cleared his throat. "Apologies, ma'am. What did you say?"

"Didn't I see you riding into town with the gold wagon today?"

He gave a reluctant nod. "Yes, ma'am, you did."

"The man riding on the other side. He looked, well...unsavory."

"Yes, ma'am. He's someone I'd recommend you stay away from."

She dabbed her mouth with a napkin, glancing at the other two men at the table. "I've seen him in town several times, never with anything other than a scowl on his face. He's always alone. Except when he's guarding the wagon, of course. I asked around, and no one knows much about him or where he's staying. I mean, there aren't many places in town besides my boardinghouse and those rooms above the Lucky Lady." She shivered as the words came out. "I don't even want to think about when those were last cleaned."

Colt stared at her, surprised Dahlia knew so much about Black.

"Anyway, Josiah..." She glanced around the table at the confused expressions. "Josiah Lloyd, who runs the post office and telegraph, told me the man had sent a letter off to someone in

Conviction. Posted it himself yesterday. I suppose everyone must have family somewhere." Setting her napkin on the table, she stood, holding up her hand when the men started to stand. "No need to get up, gentlemen. I'm just getting dessert."

While the other two men began conversing, Colt thought about what he'd learned from Dahlia. She'd given him much to think about, as well as a reason for another telegram to Brodie MacLaren. There'd been mention of a woman in Conviction, someone who might have helped Black with the attacks against the MacLarens. No one had any information on her identity.

A quick telegram could alert Brodie. The sheriff might be able to assign a deputy to watch the mail delivery, see if they might be able to identify the mystery woman. If so, he'd bet a month's pay she'd be able to tie Black to the murder of the MacLaren ranch hand and the poisoning of Circle M cattle.

Pushing away from the table, Colt surged to his feet, looking at the men across the table. "Please make my apologies to Mrs. Keach."

The photographer began to reply when the salesman interrupted him, his eyes narrowed in censure. "What reason should we give?"

Colt paused for a moment. "Tell her I'm going to track down Josiah Lloyd."

Circle M

Ewan and Ian MacLaren stood at the head of the large dining room table in Kyla's house, waiting as the family assembled. His gaze moving around the table, Ewan stopped on Blaine, while Ian's gaze landed on his son, Sean.

Quinn MacLaren hurried through the front door, removing his hat. "Sorry I'm late, Uncle Ewan. A few strays got away from me."

An amused grin appeared on Ewan's face. "Did you find them, lad?"

"Aye, sir."

"Then there's no harm." Ewan looked at his family, some faces showing concern, others curiosity, while a few looked as if they'd rather be somewhere else. "Ian and I've some news for you. As you all know, Sean has been asking to be sent home to attend school in Edinburgh. It's a long journey and the lad would be gone a long time."

"Too long in my mind," Ian interjected.

Ewan nodded. "Aye, it is." He glanced at Sean, seeing his nephew's shoulders slump. "We've discussed his wish over many glasses of whiskey."

"Too many," his wife, Lorna, murmured to Kyla, who stood next to her.

After holding up his hand to stop the snickers, Ewan placed his hands on the table, leaning forward. "We've come to the decision to let Sean go."

A loud whoop sounded at the end of the table where Sean stood with his cousins, Fletcher, Bram, and Camden. His face reddened as those close by clasped him on the shoulder and pulled him into a hug, offering congratulations.

"Your ma and I expect you to return, lad. You'll not be disappointing us." Ian scooted past everyone to wrap his arms around his son.

Clearing his throat, Sean choked on the emotion rushing through him. "Thanks, Da. I'll be coming home. You've my promise on that." He glanced toward his mother, his stomach clenching at the tears in her eyes.

"We've one more decision to announce." The room quieted, their attention back on Ewan. "This is not easy for us, but a choice Ian and I felt had to be made." His gaze locked on Blaine. "Lad, we're asking you to go to Settlers Valley to help Caleb and Heather."

Blaine's jaw clenched, eyes burning at his uncle's words. He couldn't move, his body rooted where he stood.

"They've need of your help, lad," Ian added, seeing the anger build on his nephew's face.

Except for the rustling of Kyla's skirt as she moved next to her son, the room remained silent. She placed a hand on Blaine's arm, but he shook it away, his body beginning to tremble.

He refused to make eye contact with anyone as pain washed over his face.

"Blaine. Have you nothing to say?" Ewan asked, his face clouding.

Fisting, then relaxing his hands at his sides, Blaine nodded. "Aye. I'll be leaving in the morning."

"You'll not need to be leaving before Christmas, lad."

Swallowing the bile building in his throat, Blaine met Ewan's gaze. "Aye, I do. But I'll not be going to Settlers Valley." Turning his back on his family, the people he loved most, he began to leave, stopping when Colin grabbed his arm.

"What do you mean?"

Glaring at his older brother, Blaine lifted his hand, shoving Colin aside. "You've no say on what I do any longer." Taking one last glance around the table, he nodded at his younger brother, Camden, and his cousins, Bram and Fletcher, then stormed from the house.

"Blaine, wait!" Kyla ran after him, stopping to cast a withering look at Ewan. "You've only yourself to blame for this."

The front door slammed behind her as she followed her son to the barn, slowing her pace when she saw him gathering his gear.

"Please. You can't be leaving us like this."

Almost ripping the hook from the wall as he grabbed a halter, Blaine moved past her toward the door leading to the pasture behind the barn. Whistling, he waited until Galath trotted up to him, lowering his head for Blaine to stroke.

"Where will you go?" Her voice broke, tears pooling in her eyes.

He didn't speak for several minutes as he saddled his horse. Walking to a chest, he opened the lid, taking out several boxes of ammunition. He stuffed them into his saddlebags, then grabbed a heavy coat, shoving his arms into the sleeves before turning toward his mother.

"I'm sorry, Ma, but I can't stay." He nodded toward the house. "I'll not be doing what Ewan and Ian want. Not this time."

"Don't go, lad. Not like this." She swiped at the moisture on her face.

Blaine pulled her into his arms. "I love you, Ma, but this is no longer where I belong." Kissing her cheek, he dropped his arms, picking up Galath's reins. Mounting, he looked down at his mother. "I've some money, but..."

Putting a hand to her breaking heart, Kyla shook her head. "You'll be letting me know where you are. I'll be getting money to you." She reached out, gripping his leg. "You'll not forget to be letting me know where you are?"

Blaine shook his head. "Nae, Ma. I'll not be forgetting. I wish..." His voice trailed off, his eyes showing the misery he felt.

"Wish what?"

Scrubbing a hand down his face, he looked out the large front doors to see his family gathering outside the barn. "It's not important. I'll be grabbing some clothes at Ian's, then I'm gone. Don't let anyone follow me."

Touching his heels to Galath's sides, Blaine reined the gelding out of the barn, ignoring the pleas for him to stop. Several minutes later, he stopped in front of Ian's home, gathering what he could fit into a satchel his father had given him. He couldn't help wondering how the decision might have been different if his father, the oldest of the brothers, had lived.

Ignoring the tightening in his chest, he dashed outside, securing the satchel behind the saddle. Seeing Camden, Fletcher, and Bram running toward him, he swung atop Galath, ignoring their shouts as he lifted a hand. Reining around, he moved his horse into a gallop, leaving everything he'd ever known behind.

"We need to go after him, lads." Fletcher stared after Blaine.

"Leave the lad be, Fletch. He'll not be coming back with us, no matter what we say." Camden, his chest squeezing, watched as his brother disappeared into the darkness.

Taking off his hat, Fletcher flung it to the ground. "I love my da, but he handled this all wrong with Blaine. The lad didn't know they'd made the decision before being told of it. It wasn't right."

Removing his hat, Bram raked a hand through his hair, mumbling a string of curses. "It's not often I'd be disagreeing with the uncles, but tonight is one. I agree with Fletch. The way they announced the decision wasn't right. If I were the lad, I'd be doing the same."

Camden looked at Bram. "Leaving?"

"Aye. At least long enough to clear my head."

"I'm not thinking that's what Blaine has planned." Picking up his hat, Fletcher slammed it back onto his head. "I'll not be letting him go alone." He didn't wait to hear Bram's or Camden's objections as he ran to a nearby pasture to get his horse.

Catching up to him, Camden grabbed his arm. "You can't be leaving, too."

"He'll be going to Buckie's, probably bunk down at the Gold Dust tonight. That's where I'm going. You can come with me or leave me be, but I'm going."

Bram shared a look with Camden, then stepped next to Fletcher. "I can see we'll not be changing your mind. I'm going with you."

Blowing out a frustrated breath, Camden cursed his brother for leaving and his uncles for being the reason. "You're eejits, both of you."

Bram smiled. "So you'll be riding with us?"

Shaking his head, he whistled for his horse. "Aye. There'll be hell to pay tomorrow."

Fletcher clasped his shoulder. "Then we'll deal with it tomorrow, lad."

Chapter Thirteen

Geneen stayed on the porch with Sarah and Colin, doing her best not to show the anger seething inside. She loved Blaine as a brother, the same as Colin and Camden. It didn't excuse what had happened tonight.

They could hear the aunts and uncles yelling at each other. When Blaine rode off, Kyla and the other aunts had followed Ewan home, their displeasure at the decision obvious. His wife, Lorna, sided with the others, asking him what he and Ian had been thinking, making such an announcement without speaking with Blaine first. So far, it seemed no one agreed with the choice the two men made, including Colin.

Seeing movement at the barn down by Ian's house, Geneen stood. "Where are they going?"

"Who?" Colin joined Geneen at the porch railing, watching as Camden, Bram, and Fletcher saddled their horses. "Those dunderheads. They're going after him."

Geneen turned to look at him. "Maybe you should go with them. Unless you're fine with him leaving."

"Geneen!" Sarah jumped up, moving between her sister and Colin. "Of course he doesn't want Blaine to leave. Do you?" She looked up at her husband, disappointed when he didn't respond. "Colin?"

Settling an arm over his wife's shoulders, he shook his head. "Nae, I don't want him to be leaving, and I don't agree with what the uncles did. But the lad may need time to think through their decision."

Geneen wrapped her arms around her waist. "I don't understand. Why can't he refuse to go?"

Colin glanced down at her. "It's not the way things are done here, lass."

"I've never heard of them making a decision without talking it over with those involved. They met with Sean many times about veterinary school. Did they ever talk to Blaine about what they were considering?"

Colin's mouth twisted, his gaze fixed on the three MacLarens riding out to find Blaine. "Nae, they didn't."

"They decided to send him away because of the problems between you. Right?"

His arm still around Sarah, he looked down at Geneen. "I don't know, lass. They didn't speak to me about it. Ewan and Ian didn't talk it over with anybody in the family. What I do know is I've never spoken to them about our disagreements. I thought Blaine and I'd be working it out on our own."

Sarah touched Colin's chest. "Where will he go?"

Dropping his arm, he didn't reply as he walked down the steps to stand in front of the house. Glancing back at Sarah, he shook his head. "I wish I knew, lass."

Conviction

"Another." Blaine set the empty glass on the bar, lost in his own thoughts. Anger and a sense of betrayal fought for space in his mind. He never thought Colin would turn on him as he did, going to the uncles, persuading them to send him away. They should've worked out their differences alone, as brothers. Now they might never have the chance.

"Three whiskeys."

Blaine stared down at his drink, not turning his head to acknowledge his younger brother's voice, nor the men who now flanked him. Glancing up, he looked at the mirror behind the bar, seeing Camden on his left, Fletcher and Bram on his right.

"I'll not be going back, Cam."

Sipping his whiskey, Camden shook his head. "We don't expect you to."

He glanced at his younger brother. "Then why follow me?"

Camden rolled the glass between his fingers. "What they did wasn't right."

Snorting, Blaine tossed back his second whiskey, signaling for another. "They did what Colin wanted."

"Nae. He'd never go so far as to be asking the uncles to send you away. It's not his way."

Fletcher nudged Blaine's shoulder. "Cam's right. They did this on their own without talking to the rest of the clan. I'm thinking Da and Ian don't know of the problems between you and Colin."

Blaine shook his head. "Why else would they send me away? Nae, Colin spoke with them."

Leaning across Fletcher, Bram caught Blaine's attention. "I agree with Fletch and Cam. It isn't Colin's way to be talking to the uncles about what's been happening between the two of you. The lad would've spoken with you."

Fletcher nodded. "The lad doesn't believe in settling personal disputes by bringing them to the uncles."

Drawing in a breath, Blaine cradled his glass in his hands, staring into it. "Then why?"

Fletcher waited until the bartender refilled his glass, then looked at Blaine. "They've a reason. Da and Ian don't make decisions without talking it through."

"With all the lads involved," Blaine added, underscoring the fact Ewan and Ian had never spoken with him.

The four fell silent, sipping whiskey. Blaine glanced into the mirror, spotting a new barmaid, a woman he'd never seen before. Watching as she talked to some cowhands, laughing easily, he decided she couldn't be more than seventeen or eighteen.

Blaine rarely availed himself of the saloon women. He preferred to play cards, talk with family and friends, then ride home. Something about her drew his attention in a way he'd never experienced.

As he watched her move, tendrils of shiny brown hair graced her cheeks. He had the strangest urge to brush them from her face.

"What are your plans, lad?" Fletcher waved off the bartender when he began to pour another round.

The question brought Blaine back to what he'd been avoiding—deciding what to do next. "I've not decided, other than I'll not be going back to Circle M."

Camden choked on the last of his whiskey. "Ever?"

Fletcher walked around Blaine, slapping Camden's back. "Aunt Kyla will hunt you down if she suspects you'll not be coming back."

Bram settled his back against the bar. "Aye, lad. Your ma will not be happy to learn you don't plan to return."

"I've not said I'll *never* be going back, lads." Blaine's gaze landed on the saloon girl once more, a slow grin tugging at his mouth. "I'll just not be buckling under the uncles' demands. I'm almost twenty-three, old enough to be getting a foreman's job at almost any ranch this side of the Mississippi." He clasped Fletcher on the back. "They've Colin and Quinn to lead the men, and they've decided I'm no longer needed at the ranch. Nae, they'll not be missing me."

"What of us?" Fletcher asked, not willing to let his cousin go.

"You'll be doing what you always do. My decision to leave will change nothing." Lifting his empty glass, he signaled for the bartender. "One more round, lads. Then you're off to the ranch."

Circle M

Geneen paced back and forth in front of her bedroom window, peeking out the curtains every few minutes to see if the men had returned.

Blaine leaving had shaken her. They'd been close, living in the same house since she and Sarah moved from Oregon. They were the same age, and until she'd met Nate, most days she rode alongside Blaine when tending cattle.

He and Fletcher were the ones to fetch her from Highlander Ranch. They were the same two who'd trained her horse, Gypsy, making certain she knew how to handle the young mare before surrendering the reins. She'd become close to both of them, but especially Blaine. Her heart ached at the thought of never seeing him again. The same way it burned each time she thought of Nate.

Geneen sat on the edge of the bed, staring across the room, the same as she'd done the last several nights. Sleep had been allusive since returning to Circle M, and her instincts told her tonight would be no different. Christmas loomed a few days away. She still didn't feel any excitement over the usually joyful event. Her life hadn't come back together as she'd hoped after leaving Settlers Valley.

Geneen needed to make a decision about staying or going back to Highlander Ranch. Somehow, Blaine riding off had helped clarify the choice.

Jumping up at the sound of horses, Geneen dashed to the window, pulling back the curtains.

Two men rode toward the main barn. Only two of the four who'd ridden off. She knew neither were Blaine and wondered who'd decided to stay with him, at least for tonight. Whoever it was, she knew the uncles would have severe words for him, and for Blaine, if he ever decided to come home.

Home. The word sent a rush of uncertainty through her. Geneen left her parents' home in Oregon to follow her sister to Circle M. The MacLarens became her new family, offering everything she could've imagined. They'd been happy for her when she decided to stay with Caleb and Heather, never questioning her choice or pushing for her to return.

Settling under the covers, she pulled them under her chin, closing her eyes. She'd planned to ride out to the north range tomorrow with Blaine, Fletcher, and Bram. Quinn needed one of the smaller herds moved south and wanted it done before Christmas. It would be hard driving them without Blaine. Even the smaller drives had a designated trail boss.

Tomorrow's trail boss was now miles away, headed toward a destination only he knew.

Blaine woke to bright sunlight streaming in through threadbare curtains, his head splitting. Closing his eyes, he groaned at the roiling in his stomach.

Hearing the familiar sounds of people moving along the main street, he pushed himself up, his eyes opening to slits as he gripped his head. Looking around, his gaze stopped on a familiar bright green dress hanging next to the door.

"Where the hell am I?" Blaine mumbled, trying to remember how he came to be here. Before he could wonder too long, the door opened, a woman backing into the room with a tray in her hands. His breath caught the instant she turned to face him.

"Oh. I didn't know you'd woken up. I'll just set this down and go."

He raked a hand through his hair, unable to form words with her so close. Her brown hair had been piled into a bun on top of her head, her blue cotton dress not close to the green outfit she wore the night before.

The girl from the saloon stood inches away, and he sat there with a blinding headache, churning stomach, and mouth refusing to open. Blaine watched as she reached into a pocket of her dress, removing a packet.

"Doc Tilden said you might need this." As she set the pouch of headache medicine on the table, she noticed his shirt open to the waist, his strong muscles rippling as he swung his feet to the floor. "I, um...should leave you alone."

"Nae. Wait." Blaine held up a hand for her to stop. "Where am I?"

She glanced around, her face flushing as she did her best not to look at him. "In my room at the Gold Dust."

Closing his eyes, he tried again to remember what happened after the lads left for the ranch. Opening them, he saw her inch toward the door. "How did I get here?"

"Well...you and your friend were almost falling down when you left Buckie's. You'd been shouting, shoving each other..." She bit her lip, stifling a giggle. "Anyway, someone sent for the sheriff. You collapsed on the boardwalk. Your friend walked the other way and collapsed in the street. When Sheriff MacLaren arrived, he, um...well, he cursed a bit, then pulled your friend up and hauled him away. He didn't see you."

Blaine didn't think he could feel more miserable. Pinching the bridge of his nose, he groaned. A dim memory began to form, then crystalize. Fletcher had decided to stay behind when Camden and Bram rode home. He'd kept Blaine company at the bar, telling jokes until they were both too full of whiskey to think. Stumbling outside, he'd gone one way while Fletcher went the other, looking for their horses. Brodie must've been furious when he had to haul his brother out of the street.

Rubbing his eyes, he looked at the girl. "How did I end up here?"

Settling her hand on the door handle, she turned away when he stood, his shirt falling open, his pants unbuttoned.

Noticing her discomfort, Blaine quickly fastened his pants and buttoned his shirt. "Sorry, lass. You can turn around now."

Glancing over her shoulder, she tightened her grip on the door. "Two men from the saloon came out and saw me bending over you. I think they may have known you." She shook her head slightly. "I told them you could stay here for the night." Slipping a strand of hair behind her ear, she cleared her throat, pointing to the tray. "There's some food for you. I need to get back to work."

Blaine glanced at the food, then back at her, his gaze narrowing. "I thought you were one of the saloon girls at Buckie's." Seeing her face flush again, a grin split his face.

Crossing her arms, she glared at him, raising her chin. "I only serve drinks there when one of the girls is sick, and that's *all* I do at Buckie's. I clean rooms here at the Gold Dust two days a week and serve meals in their restaurant most days. This room comes as part of my pay."

"Apologies, lass. I didn't mean to offend you."

"I'm sure you didn't. Now, I must get back to my work."

"Wait."

She let out a frustrated breath. "What now?"

"What's your name, lass? It's hard to thank someone when I'm not knowing their name."

She licked her lips. "Permilia," she whispered.

Blinking, he leaned closer. "What?"

"My name. It's Permilia. Friends back home call me Lia."

Stepping closer, he held out his hand. "It's nice to meet you, Lia. I'm Blaine."

Reluctantly, she gripped his hand. "Hello, Blaine." She looked at their joined hands. Before he could say any more, she let go, turning the knob before rushing out.

He wanted to call after her to stop, thank her again for helping him. Instead, he stared down at his rumpled clothes, then moved to the mirror. Wincing at the sight, he chuckled, surprised she hadn't run out sooner.

Sitting on the bed, he picked up a piece of toast from the tray. Chewing, he thought of Lia, letting her name roll around in his head, liking the way it sounded when he whispered it to himself.

Finishing the eggs and coffee, he walked to the dresser, splashing water on his face. He began to feel a little more human. A pounding on the door caused him to pause. Lia wouldn't bother to knock, and no one else knew he was here.

"Open up, Blaine."

Grimacing at Brodie's voice, knowing there was no point stalling, he opened the door, staring at the scowl on his cousin's face.

"Brodie. How did you know I was here?"

Pushing past him, Brodie didn't answer as he looked around, then placed fisted hands on his hips. "I heard Lia had you brought here, so I came to find out what the hell is going on. Fletcher's still passed out at my house."

"You know Lia?"

"We'll speak of the lass later. Right now, I want to know what you and Fletcher would be doing in town, getting drunk in the middle of the week." Brodie grabbed the only chair in the room, turning it around to sit, his arms resting on the back.

Staring at him for a moment, Blaine eased himself down onto the bed, resting his head in his hands. "You've not heard?"

Brodie's features relaxed. "I've heard nothing, lad."

Dropping his hands, he rested his arms on his knees. "I've left Circle M."

"Why?"

Standing, Blaine paced to the only window in the room. "The uncles decided to send me to work with Caleb and Heather. They never spoke of it to me. Instead, they gathered the family and made their announcement. What your da and Ian did wasn't right. It's not the way we do things."

Brodie rubbed his chin. "They never spoke to you of what they were thinking?"

"Nae, not a word. They told Sean he'd be going to Scotland, then said I'd be leaving for Settlers Valley." Turning from the window, he glowered at Brodie. "I'll not be joining Caleb and Heather, and I'll not be going back to Circle M. I'm leaving."

Opening his mouth to reply, he stopped when the door opened, a red-eyed Fletcher standing in the hall. Walking inside, he closed the door, leaning a shoulder against it, his gaze going to Brodie.

"Did he tell you?"

Brodie nodded. "Aye."

"And what would you be thinking about it?"

"I'm thinking the same as Blaine." He looked at his cousin. "Da and Ian made a mistake announcing a decision before speaking to you, lad."

"Then you'll be understanding why I must leave."

Brodie shook his head. "Nae. I didn't say that."

"The uncles made it clear I'm not needed at Circle M."

"There must be more to it, Blaine. Da wouldn't be making this kind of decision without a good reason."

Fletcher straightened, looking at his brother. "There's more, Brodie. He's thinking Colin spoke to Da and Ian about the troubles between them." Everyone seemed to know about the altercations between Colin and Blaine—except the uncles.

He shook his head. "Nae. Colin would've talked to you, not Da and Ian. There must be another reason."

His head spinning, Blaine sat on the bed. "I've not been able to think of one."

Brodie stood, placing a hand on Blaine's shoulder. "Then you'll need to be asking them."

"Nae. The uncles should've spoken with me, told me their reasons. It's the way of it with the MacLarens." Standing, Blaine grabbed his gunbelt from the table, strapping it around his waist. "I'm leaving for a time. I'll let you know where I am, but I'll not be returning to Circle M...not for a while."

Murmuring a curse, Brodie tried once more. "If you're determined to leave, give it a few days. Stay with me and Maggie. You leaving isn't right, lad."

Picking up his hat, Blaine settled it on his head. Maybe his cousins were right and he should take time to think through his decision. Plus, the extra days would give him time to learn more about Lia.

"If I stay, I've a condition for you."

Brodie lifted a brow. "Which is?"

"You'll be telling me what you know about Lia."

Chapter Fourteen

Settlers Valley

Black smiled. Nettles had finalized the schedule. Right after Christmas would be the biggest load yet, and it would mark Black's last shipment before leaving for good. He'd make a brief stop in Conviction, then head toward Montana where he planned to start over.

They'd made three gold runs to town, the last one that morning, proving to Nettles and Polk he and his men could be trusted.

The two men he'd hired did their job well, guns ready while keeping watch on the trail ahead. The driver had worked for Nettles as long as he'd owned the mine. He'd once told Black nothing exciting ever happened during the gold runs to town.

That was about to change.

Conviction

"We've had a deputy watching the postal deliveries for several days and nothing from Settlers Valley. Ira Greene assured me he'd notify one of us if a letter arrived. Are you sure Colt understood the town right?" Sam leaned forward, resting his arms on his thighs as he watched

Brodie put the wanted posters back in the top drawer.

"Aye. His telegram was specific. Maybe the person giving him the information was wrong." Brodie had received the telegram over a week ago, alerting them to watch for a letter from Settlers Valley. "Colt guessed the recipient might be the lass connected to Black."

"What do you want to do?"

Brodie rubbed a hand over his day-old beard. "Confirm with Ira he'll be notifying us of any mail from Settlers Valley. Make certain he knows it's urgent. We'll not be posting any more deputies."

They both turned as the door opened. "Ah, the two gentlemen I wanted to see." Bayard Donahue strolled in, placing his black cowboy hat on a hook next to Brodie's.

"Good morning, Bay. Pour some coffee and sit down." Brodie nodded to a chair next to Sam.

Bay grabbed a cup, filling it partway before taking a sip, grimacing. "Lordy. How do you drink this?"

Chuckling, Sam put his cup to his mouth and took a big gulp. Shrugging, he looked at Bay. "Tastes all right to me."

Shooting Sam an indignant glare, Bay walked to the back door, tossing the contents of his cup outside.

Pointing to the chair, Brodie grinned. "Stop complaining and tell us why you're here."

Settling into a chair, Bay crossed one leg over the other, steepling his fingers under his chin. "Your father and Ian have hired me to draw up a contract to purchase property between here and Settlers Valley. I'll need to ride up there to speak with the owners and check the boundaries. I know you've a man up there checking into Black Jolly and thought I'd see if you wanted me to carry a message to him."

Brodie's lips parted, his eyes widening. "So I'm understanding you, Da and Ian plan to purchase land north of here?"

Bay's expression changed to one of concern. "They've already agreed on the prices. You hadn't heard?"

His jaw clenching, Brodie shook his head. "Nae. They've said nothing to me. Do you know if they've been talking to the other lads?"

Shifting in his seat, Bay glanced at Sam before his gaze returned to Brodie. "I don't know. They asked August to handle the transactions, but he's been doing some work for a family in San Francisco. He asked me to take care of it."

Tempering the anger rising inside, Brodie took a deep breath. "When did they talk to August?"

Clearing his throat, Bay leaned forward. "Perhaps three months ago. The purchase involves more than one property. Ewan told me he has a contact in Settlers Valley who provided names of ranchers and landowners interested in selling. When they pieced it all together, they found a way to grow Circle M by tens of thousands of acres."

"And you don't know if they've said anything to the other family members?" Sam's wife was Brodie's younger sister. He knew Jinny would've told him about something as significant as Bay described.

"I'd expect Brodie and Jinny to know about it." Leaning back in his chair, Bay rubbed a hand over his face. "Isn't it unusual for the uncles to make a decision of this scope without consulting with the rest of the family?"

Brodie nodded. "Aye. It is." Standing, he slipped on his coat. "When do you plan to leave for Settlers Valley?"

"I'd planned to go right after Christmas." Bay joined Brodie by the door. "Why?"

Ignoring Bay's question, Brodie looked at Sam. "I'm going to find Blaine and ride to Circle M. I'll be needing you to take over while I'm gone." He looked at Bay. "And you'll be riding with us."

Finding Blaine hadn't been hard. Convincing him to leave his table at the Gold Dust, where his server was Lia, proved to be a challenge. When Brodie and Bay walked into the restaurant, Lia stood at Blaine's table, pouring more coffee and smiling at something he'd said.

"I don't know where you're going to put more food. You've already had two breakfasts and four cups of coffee."

Smiling at her, Blaine leaned back in his chair. "You let me be worrying about that, lass."

Clearing his throat to get his cousin's attention, Brodie looked at Lia. "Would you mind getting two more cups of coffee?"

Flushing at being caught dallying, she moved away. "Of course, Sheriff."

Sitting down, Brodie ignored the irritation on Blaine's face. "We have to talk, lad."

"That's what I was doing before you interrupted."

Bay shook his head, suppressing a smile.

"This is important."

Blaine took a good look at Brodie's face, seeing a seriousness he'd missed when his cousin sat down. "I'm listening."

Once Lia delivered their coffee, Brodie relayed what Bay had told him. Blaine didn't interrupt, even as the muscles in his jaw clenched more with each word. When his cousin finished, he reached into his pocket, pulling out enough money to pay for everything. Picking up his hat, he nodded at Lia, unable to form a smile. He looked at Brodie.

"The uncles have a good deal of explaining to do."

"What is it you want to be speaking to your da about?" Lorna, Brodie's mother, handed him a cup of coffee, glancing at Blaine and Bay sitting across the dining room table.

His face softened from the scowl she'd first seen when the three entered the house. "It'd be best if we spoke to Da first, Ma. It isn't a simple matter."

"Is it about Blaine?" She took a seat next to him, cradling her own cup.

Brodie nodded. "It could be. We've many questions."

"Well, he and Ian will be back soon. I've not known either to miss a meal." She offered a weak smile, resting a hand on her son's shoulder for a moment before her gaze landed on Blaine. "Ewan and I are not agreeing on what happened. He and

Ian made a mistake not speaking with you, lad. I hope you'll ask them why and decide to stay."

Staring into his cup, he shook his head. "Nae, Aunt Lorna. I'll not be staying, no matter what they tell me. They don't need me here. It's the reason they want me to work with Caleb and Heather."

"It can't be what you're thinking, lad. I know it's appearing that way, but Ewan knows your skills and love of ranching. There's a reason for their decision. I'm certain of it."

His aunt's words matched those of others. Blaine wished he had as much confidence about what they believed. If the uncles had only spoken with him first...The front door opening stopped the progression of his thoughts.

"Lorna, I'm back." Ewan didn't notice those at the table as he unstrapped his gunbelt, hanging it on a hook. Turning, his grin fell when he saw the faces staring at him. Walking toward them, he extended his hand to Bay, nodding at Blaine and his son.

"I'll get you some coffee, Ewan." Standing, Lorna offered Blaine an encouraging smile.

"Thank you, Lorna." He pulled out a chair, resting his arms on the table. "You've come to talk?" He glanced at Bay, but directed his question to his son.

"Aye, Da. We've questions for you."

"If you've spoken with Bay, then I'm certain you have."

Brodie gave his father an unapologetic look. "Bay stopped by the jail to let me know he'd be riding north to draw up paperwork on property you and Ian are buying. Is it true, Da?"

Ewan nodded. "Aye. Bay has no reason to lie." He waited while Lorna placed coffee in front of him. "Sit down, love. You should be hearing this, too." Staring at the cup, he let the coffee cool before taking a sip. "When we made the deal with Archie Galloway, he spoke of other properties that might interest us. Ranchers, friends of his, were struggling and looking to sell. Ian and I met with August Fielder, thinking he might be interested in another partnership."

"He wasn't?" Brodie asked.

Ewan shook his head. "Nae, but he helped us look into the properties. He learned there were several ranchers ready to sell at a good price. August recommended Bay work on negotiations, but suggested we say nothing to the family."

"Why would he be suggesting such a thing, Da? We always talk over all big decisions."

"I know, Brodie. This time was different. August learned a group of buyers from San Francisco were looking for land in the area. If we were serious about buying, we needed to keep it private, even from family, until deals could be reached." He looked at Blaine. "I'm sorry, lad. We should've been talking to you, even if August told us not to."

"I'm not understanding what you're telling me, Uncle Ewan."

Leaning forward, Ewan clasped his hands on the table. "You're an important reason why we're believing we can buy the land."

Blaine's brows knit in confusion, but he remained silent.

"You've become a fine rancher, understanding the business and the cattle. The men respect you and you work hard, never ignoring your duties. When the sale is final, we'll be needing a lad we can trust to run the operation. That's why we want you at Highlander Ranch. You're the lad we want to be leading the additional lands."

Bay rode back to town, going straight to the jail, letting Sam know of the conversation. Ewan had called another family meeting for that evening, and Sam and Jinny were expected to be there.

By the time they arrived at Circle M, almost everyone had congregated at Kyla's. The only two missing were Colin and Quinn. Those at the earlier meeting with Ewan agreed to say nothing, leaving the explanation to the elders.

Blaine stood in the living room with Camden, Fletcher, and Bram, his gaze wandering to the door every few minutes. No one questioned his presence, which made waiting for his older brother much easier. Laughter from outside drew Blaine's attention to the entry, seeing Quinn enter. His stomach tightened when Colin followed a moment later.

He had no idea what to expect from his brother. They hadn't been on good terms for months, and after storming out, Colin hadn't come after him the way Bram had. Seeing Colin's gaze move across the room, landing on him, Blaine stilled.

"Ach, lad. You decided to come home." Colin strolled up to him, pulling him close for a quick hug. "It's good you're here."

Breaking apart, they looked at each other, Blaine's throat working as he struggled to form words. "Aye, it is."

"Since you've all arrived, Ian and I need to be explaining our actions over the last few months."

No one interrupted as Ewan explained what happened and their reasons for not including

Blaine in the decision to send him north. When finished, the family stayed silent for several moments before Colin spoke up.

"I'm understanding why August urged you to say nothing, but you should've been including some of us. Were you thinking we couldn't be trusted?"

"Nae, Colin, it wasn't that. If we had to be doing it again, we would've spoke to you, Quinn, and Brodie. And we'd have talked to Blaine. August is a good man who thought the suggestion sound."

"MacLarens aren't like most families, Da."

"I know, Fletcher. Ian and I thought we'd made a good decision. It wasn't. We'll not be doing it again."

Colin turned to Blaine. The corners of his mouth slid upwards as he clasped him on the back. "Congratulations, lad. It's a good decision, even though we'll miss you."

Across the room, Geneen approached Ewan, glancing at Colin and Blaine. She'd yet to congratulate him. First, she had her own announcement to make.

"Uncle Ewan?"

Turning, he put an arm around her. "Aye, lass."

"This may not be the time, but I want you and Uncle Ian to know I'll be returning to Settlers Valley with Blaine after Christmas."

He dropped his arm from around her shoulders. "You're not happy being back?"

"It isn't that." She glanced away, then looked back at Ewan. "It's just, well...I know how much Caleb and Heather need help. The decision to leave them was selfish."

He studied her a moment, seeing the sincerity on her face. "Nae, lass, you're not selfish. You needed to see Sarah and the rest of your family. Nothing wrong with that."

"You aren't angry about me leaving?"

"Nae. You're right. They need you, and Blaine won't be there too long. It's a good decision. Have you told Sarah?"

Geneen nodded. "Yes, and she understands."

"Good. Then if you've no objection, I'll be telling the others." When she shook her head, he turned toward the others, clearing his throat. "I've one more thing to tell you." While the voices quieted, he looked down at her. "You're certain, lass?"

Pushing aside any doubts, she nodded.

"Seems Geneen's been missing Highlander Ranch. When Blaine leaves, she'll be riding with him."

A loud whoop followed a few moments of surprised silence. Blaine strode across the room, taking Geneen in his arms and swinging her around. Setting her on the floor, he settled an arm across her shoulders.

"I can't think of anyone else I'd rather be riding alongside me."

Laughing, she placed a kiss on Blaine's cheek. "We'll see what you say by the time we reach the ranch."

Chapter Fifteen

Highlander Ranch

The fire crackled, illuminating the pine tree Heather had decorated with berries and brightly colored ribbon. She walked in from the kitchen, going straight to Caleb, who sat in his favorite chair, nursing a cup of hot cocoa. Sitting on the arm of the chair, she wrapped her arms around his neck and kissed him.

Nate had seen them do this many times. On Christmas night, the sight tugged a little harder on his heart.

Taking a sip of his own cocoa, he stared into the fire, the flames reminding him of how much Geneen loved this time of year. Then again, she loved all times of year. Each season brought new experiences, allowed her to grow in a way her father had never allowed. He recalled the day she'd told him of her loving mother and distant, domineering father.

Dougal MacGregor had been hard on his wife and three daughters, expecting much and giving little. When he demanded Sarah marry a man not of her choosing, her sister revolted, leaving their home to find work in their small Oregon town. Sarah had vowed to wait for Colin and nothing could dissuade her. When Sarah followed Colin to Circle M, Geneen left with them, never looking back. Those lessons taught her much.

Strong and loyal, she never complained, no matter the odds against her. Nate loved everything about her. Soon, he'd be riding back to Circle M to claim what he believed to be his.

"Did you hear from your parents, Nate?"

Shaking his head slightly to rid himself of his thoughts, he nodded at Caleb. "I received a letter this week. They're doing fine, which is a relief after Pa's illness last summer."

"They must be missing you very much at Christmas."

"Yes, they do, Heather. I hope to go out there in a few months for a visit."

Until this moment, Nate hadn't made a decision. The thought of returning to Pennsylvania no longer bothered him. He'd come a long way since riding away from his family's Harrisburg ranch. The need to return, show them he'd recovered mentally and physically, tugged at him. If she agreed, he'd take Geneen with him. He knew his family would love her as much as he did.

"I'm glad Colt joined us for supper today."

Nate forced himself back to the present. Caleb and Heather knew about Colt and his history with Nate when they'd both been in Nacogdoches. They knew only of the friendship, not that he'd come to Settlers Valley as a U.S. Marshal looking for Black Jolly.

He nodded at Heather, a grin tugging at the corners of his mouth. "I know he appreciated the invitation."

"The lad should've stayed the night instead of riding back to town."

Nate didn't reply to Heather's comment. He knew Colt felt compelled to return to town with the hope Jolly would be looking for him. He understood there'd be at least one more shipment, but as yet, Black hadn't told him the date.

And the instant Colt knew, he'd tell Nate.

Circle M

"I'm going to miss you, Geneen." Sarah swiped tears from her face, watching as her sister packed the last item in her satchel and secured it to the saddle. "Letters would be good." She tried to smile, failing miserably.

"I'll do my best, but you know how much I hate to write."

"I do." Sarah wrapped her arms around Geneen, hugging her. Pulling away, she kissed her cheek. "You'll be back in the spring, though, right?"

"Of course I will. Maybe sooner, now that we know a shorter trail."

"You ready, lass?" Blaine walked toward them with his horse, Galath. He looked to the east, seeing the sun rising above the mountains.

"I am."

"You sure you don't want to be staying one more day?" Colin stopped next to Blaine, holding Grant in one arm, a package in the other. "Ma wrapped food for you."

Taking the package, Blaine slipped it inside the saddlebags, turning back to Colin. "It's the day after Christmas. No sense putting it off any longer."

Colin nodded. "Aye. I'd be doing the same. Does Caleb know you're coming?"

"Nae. Ewan said he didn't send word."

Geneen stepped next to them. "There won't be a problem, Colin. Caleb and Heather will be happy to have us, and they've plenty of room."

As they stood talking, more of the family came to join them. Camden hugged them both, as did Bram and Fletcher.

"We'll be missing you, lad." Camden clasped him on the shoulder.

Smiling, Blaine shook his head. "Nae. You'll be too busy keeping the ranch going without me and Geneen."

"He's right, Cam," Fletcher joked. "At least now we'll be knowing where he'll be."

"And Caleb won't be allowing him to be a sloth," Bram added, receiving a slight shove from Blaine.

Geneen laughed at their antics, knowing how much she'd miss seeing them together. "I can confirm Caleb will expect him to work from sunup to sunset every day."

"If all goes well, he won't be having him for long." Ewan stopped beside them, followed by Ian and their wives. "Bay hopes to be having the contracts signed soon." He looked up, seeing a rider approaching. "Ah. There's the lad now."

Bay rode toward them, lifting his hand in a brief wave.

"If he hadn't come soon, we'd be riding away without him." Blaine returned the wave, then swung up and into the saddle.

Geneen gave Sarah one more hug before mounting Gypsy.

"Be safe," Sarah called after her as she reined her horse around. "Love you."

Looking over her shoulder, Geneen smiled, blowing a kiss to them all.

"My instincts tell me tomorrow's shipment is the one." Colt glanced behind him at the street, confirming no one had followed him to the livery. Black had seen him coming out of the boardinghouse, stopping him long enough to provide the news of tomorrow's trip.

Nate stood, straightening his back. "Why?"

Colt's mouth tilted into an indulgent grin. "He told me it would be the largest shipment so far."

Nate's eyes crinkled, although his features remained stoic. "If you're right, your journey may end tomorrow." He wiped his hands down his pants. "What time?"

"We leave the mine at nine o'clock."

"I'll let Marcus know."

Nate hadn't said a word to his boss about his absence during the first two shipments. When nothing happened, he felt compelled to share the reason for being gone. He shouldn't have been surprised when Marcus supported his actions, volunteering to ride out with him. Nate declined, reminding him of his responsibility to his sister.

"Did Black stay in town?"

Colt glanced over his shoulder once more. "Disappeared the same as he always does. He must have a place somewhere close because he's not at Dahlia's or in one of the rooms at the Lucky Lady."

"Good. I promised Heather I'd be at the ranch for supper. How about going to the restaurant for dinner?"

Colt pursed his lips, shaking his head once. "I'd like to, but Jolly could return at any time. I don't want him to see us together."

Marcus sauntered outside, wiping his blackened hands on a rag. "Esther has food ready and expects both of you inside the house in five minutes."

Nate chuckled. "Appears we'll be sharing a meal anyway. I doubt Black would be able to see you inside the house."

"No. I don't suppose he would."

"Miss Kamm, this is the best meatloaf I've had in a long time. But don't be telling Mrs. Keach or she might throw me out of the boardinghouse." Colt took another bite before scooping up a forkful of potatoes.

"Mrs. Keach's food is understood to be some of the best around, so I'll take that as a high compliment, Mr. Dye."

"I'd appreciate it if you'd call me Colt."

Her face flushed on a nod. "Then I expect you to call me Esther."

Marcus looked back and forth between the two, saying nothing, his brows furrowing.

"Colt is right, Esther. This is wonderful, as are all your meals." Nate took another slice of meatloaf from the platter, his hand stilling at a loud pounding on the door.

Marcus glanced around the table, his gaze stopping on Esther. "I'm not expecting anyone. Are you?"

Shaking her head, she started to stand.

"I'll get it." Marcus stood as another round of pounding began. "Hold on. I'm coming." Pulling open the door, his stern features softened when he recognized the man before him. "MacLaren, right?"

Blaine offered his hand, a grin splitting his face. "Aye. Blaine MacLaren." He stepped aside. "This is Bay Donahue, and I believe you know Geneen." Shaking Bay's hand, Marcus nodded a greeting to Geneen, hearing movement behind him.

Nate strode up to the door, his eyes widening. "Blaine? What are you doing in..." The remaining words died on his tongue when he spotted Geneen. Sucking in a breath, he recovered within seconds, clasping Blaine on the shoulder, then shaking hands with Bay. Dropping his hand, he moved forward, his gaze unwavering. "It's good to see you, Geneen." It came out as a whisper, his voice rough.

She looked him up and down, her mouth parting on a soft sigh. "Nate. You look, well...good."

A self-deprecating smile twisted his lips. "Thanks. You look beautiful."

Touching a hand to her hair, she chuckled. "It appears your eyes have suffered since I left."

He shook his head. "Not even a little, Geneen."

Marcus motioned everyone inside. "We're just having dinner. Please, sit down and join us. This is my sister, Esther, and our friend, Colt Dye."

Esther greeted everyone before hurrying into the kitchen to gather the remaining meatloaf and potatoes, thankful she always prepared extra. Returning to the dining room, she set the food down, seeing plates already in front of the guests.

Geneen noticed the woman's flushed face and felt a pang of guilt. "I hope this isn't putting you out."

"Oh, it's no trouble at all. Other than Nate, Marcus and I seldom have company. Please, help yourself and take as much as you want."

Blaine didn't hesitate to fill his plate. Bay and Geneen held back a little, then filled theirs, digging into the meal.

"This is bonny," Blaine mumbled as he swallowed a bite of meatloaf.

Geneen sent him a warning glance. "Blaine. Your manners."

Shrugging, he scooped up another forkful. "Well, it is."

Nodding, Geneen looked at Esther. "He's right. You'll have to give me your recipe."

"I'd love to share it. Our mother got it from my grandmother, made some adjustments, then gave it to me."

"And Esther made her own improvements." Marcus winked at his sister. "As she always does."

Nate couldn't stop watching Geneen for more than a few seconds. He knew they all noticed, but he didn't care. He'd missed her even more than he thought. Every part of him wanted to take her hand, lead her outside, and apologize for all he'd done to hurt her. Now wasn't the time. If she'd let him, he'd find the right time as soon as they took care of Black. Nate forced himself to look across the table at his friend.

"What are you doing here, Blaine?"

He nodded at Bay. "He's the one who should be telling you."

Bay set down his fork and picked up his cup of coffee to wash down the food before explaining. After several minutes, he shared a look with the others at the table.

"It's important you speak of this to no one. The MacLarens have kept their intentions quiet for months. I'd hate to see this not work out because other buyers have heard the properties are for sale."

Nate shifted toward Bay, nodding. "I can assure you, no one at this table will say a word."

Marcus looked at Esther and Colt. "He's right, Bay. You can trust us to keep quiet."

Blaine leaned forward in his chair, sipping his coffee. "Since I'm new here, is there anything exciting going on?"

Nate, Marcus, and Colt shared a look before Nate spoke. "Well, there is a small matter about a gold shipment."

Colt explained about the gold mine, the people involved, and the shipments. When finished, he rested his arms on the table. "The town is more interesting than I first imagined."

"Black Jolly?" Blaine looked at Geneen and Bay. "He's the man who carried out Giles

Delacroix's orders. The man who killed our ranch hand."

Bay nodded. "I remember the name from the statements Giles made."

Colt crossed his arms. "As I said, he's wanted for other crimes in Texas."

He looked at Colt. "And you're the U.S. Marshal sent to take him back."

"I am."

"Are you required to take him back to Texas?" Bay asked, warming to the subject.

Colt tilted his head a little, a glint in his eyes. "If I can arrest him for crimes here, there's a chance we can try him in Settlers Valley."

Bay rubbed his chin. "Or in Conviction, if there's enough evidence." He looked at Nate. "You know, it might be he'd be sent to San Francisco for trial."

Nate shook his head. "We've transported a few other prisoners there. They seem much more forgiving of crimes than any jury in Conviction. I'd rather see him tried closer to home."

Bay looked at Colt. "You said the next shipment is tomorrow?"

Colt nodded. "We leave the mine about nine o'clock."

"I'll be keeping watch on the wagon," Nate said.

Geneen clasped her hands in her lap, a grim expression on her face. "Only you, Nate?"

He nodded. "I've seen Colt in action. The two of us will be enough."

Bay looked at Colt. "What if there are others? People who are helping Black?"

"From all I've seen, the man is working alone."

Blaine narrowed his gaze on Nate. "What if he's not?"

Geneen nodded. "He had a gang in Conviction. There must have been close to fifteen men working for him. I believe Colt mentioned Black had men working with him in Texas."

Colt looked around the table. "We caught those men. Only Black got away. And from what I've seen, there aren't many men in this town who'd go along with his plan. They're ranchers, farmers, and businessmen. They've families." He shook his head. "I don't think we need to worry about Black having any more than the other guard and the driver."

"The driver was hired by Nettles," Nate added.

"Are you willing to bet your lives on it?" Bay asked.

Colt and Nate looked at each other, remaining silent.

"I'm not thinking so." Blaine glanced at Bay, his brow lifting. "Are you up for a little excitement, lad?"

A wry grin tugged at Bay's lips. "Always."

Blaine returned the grin. "It's settled then, lads. Now, tell us the details."

Chapter Sixteen

Highlander Ranch

Caleb walked out of the barn and stopped at the sight of three riders coming toward him. "What's this?" A smile spread across his face when he recognized them. Opening his arms, he wrapped Geneen in a hug the instant she slid from the saddle. Letting her go, he stepped back. "This is a wonderful surprise."

She felt a ripple of nerves. "I hope you don't mind me returning."

"I just hope you're here to stay. Heather will be thrilled." Caleb gave Blaine a hug, then shook hands with Bay. "Good to see both of you."

"Ewan sent me to help you and Heather. I'll be staying for a while." Blaine saw his brows knit together. Clasping him on the shoulder, he sought to relieve the confusion on Caleb's face. "It's an exciting reason I'm here. We'll be explaining everything to you and Heather."

"Whatever the reason, you're always welcome. Heather should be coming along in a bit. She stopped to check on a new calf in our eastern pasture. Have you had dinner?"

Geneen nodded. "We stopped to let Nate know we were back."

Caleb's brow lifted. "I'll wager it was quite a surprise for him. I hope it went better this time."

She let out a half-hearted chuckle. "He didn't walk away from me if that's what you mean."

Settling an arm over her shoulders, Caleb grabbed Gypsy's reins, walking toward the barn. "He's not the same as when you left. These last few weeks have made a big difference in the way he sees himself."

A knot formed in her stomach. "Then leaving turned out for the best."

He shook his head. "Not in the way you may be thinking." Stopping at a stall, he unsaddled the mare, settling it on a rack, while Blaine and Bay removed the tack from their horses. "It's for the two of you to work out. All I'm saying is you might consider giving him a chance."

Letting out a breath, she nodded. "I've also changed since leaving."

Leading the way to the house, an impish grin slipped across Caleb's face. "I hope not too much."

"Geneen!" Heather whipped her hat off her head, waving it in the air. Reining Shamrock to a stop, she jumped to the ground, running toward them. "You're back." Giving her a hug, she stepped away. "How long?"

Geneen couldn't help the happiness flowing through her. "For as long as you'll put up with me." She looked over Heather's shoulder, seeing Blaine and Bay striding toward them. "I didn't come alone."

Whipping around, Heather whooped at the sight of her cousin. "Blaine. I should've been knowing you'd be the one to be riding here with her." She hugged him. "And Bay. It's been a while." After giving him a brief hug, she slipped an arm through Blaine's. "Let's get in the house and you can be telling us all about the family. Have you had dinner?"

The three let out simultaneous chuckles. "Aye, at the Kamm's," Blaine told her. "We wanted to see Nate before riding out. We met an interesting man. Colt Dye. Do you know him?"

They walked up the steps and into the house, hanging their coats on hooks by the door. "Aye. Colt is an old friend of Nate's. Caleb and I know little about him, other than he guards gold shipments from the mine to town."

Blaine and Bay shared a look before Blaine gave a slight shake of his head.

"I've lemonade and coffee in the kitchen." Heather glanced at the men. "Unless you'd like something stronger."

"Coffee is fine," Bay replied.

Blaine nodded. "The same for me."

"I'll have lemonade. No one makes it better than Heather." Geneen removed her hat, running her hands over her tousled hair. She followed Heather into the kitchen while the men took seats in the living room.

Bay looked around the spacious room. He hadn't expected something this nice or as large. "This is a fine place you have here, Caleb."

Leaning back, he placed an arm across the back of the sofa. "Archie Galloway built it years ago, expecting to have several children. His wife died during childbirth and he never remarried." He nodded toward the side of the house. "He lives in the foreman's home."

Bay nodded. "I saw it. It's a good size."

Caleb snorted. "Archie doesn't do anything small. I'll make sure you meet him while you're here."

"I'd like that." Bay didn't mention he'd corresponded with Archie several times about expanding the MacLaren ranch. He'd yet to meet the man.

"Here you are." Heather set a tray on the table, making room for the plate of sliced sorghum cake Geneen placed beside it. "This is all the lads left of the cake from Christmas. It's Ma's recipe."

Blaine reached out to grab a slice, unapologetic at his enthusiasm. "Aunt Audrey makes grand sorghum cake." He took a bite, closing his eyes as he chewed. "Ah, lass, this is grand. Your ma would be proud of you."

Caleb sipped his coffee, impatience pounding through him as he waited for the reason Ewan sent Blaine to join them.

"I'm sure you want to be knowing why Bay and I are here."

Heather looked at Caleb, tilting her head to the side, then turned toward Blaine. "I thought you were just escorting Geneen. Is there more to it?"

"Aye, lass, there is." Swallowing the last of the cake, he picked up his coffee, going through the same conversation they'd had with the others. When finished, Heather's face held a wary expression, while Caleb let out a low whistle.

"You don't like the idea, Heather?" Bay asked.

She shook her head. "It's not that. I'm wondering if the family has the funds for such an ambitious purchase."

It was Blaine who answered. "Ewan and Ian showed us documents from the bank. The family is doing quite well from investments made with August in San Francisco. You may not remember, but before Da and Uncle Gillis died, the family purchased property not far from the center of town. Tenants occupy several buildings, bringing in a good deal of money. The cattle contracts are lucrative as well."

"And don't we own land in Conviction?" Heather asked Blaine.

"Aye. Several buildings and houses. Most are in partnership with August. Those are the funds allowing Sean to attend veterinary school and to purchase the property."

Caleb stood, walking to the window and pulling back the drapery to look outside. He turned to look at Bay. "It's still a risk. Do any of the properties include livestock?"

Bay reached into a pocket, pulling out a folded paper. Standing, he walked to the dining room table, spreading it out to reveal a map. He waited until the others gathered around. Pointing to the areas circled, Bay explained the different ranches and farms.

"Each of the properties include livestock, although each is different. For instance, this farm raises pigs, chickens, and turkeys. They have a few dairy cows, but no cattle, and only two horses for riding and two for pulling the plow and wagon. They're leaving it all, as they plan to take the steamship to Sacramento and buy a store."

Bay circled his finger around another property. "This is a working cattle ranch. The owners are Archie's age. They have two daughters, both married and living in San Francisco. The couple wants to join them. It includes a few hundred head of cattle and at least a dozen horses. There's a bunkhouse, large barn, and two-story house. This is where Ewan and Ian plan to have the main ranch house. It's where Blaine will be living."

Heather looked at Caleb. "How far away are you thinking it is from here, lad?"

Caleb studied the map, then shrugged. "No more than an hour's ride. It's close to the lake where we encountered the Maidu Indian boy. It would be a simple matter to get to Settlers Valley and back in a few hours." He indicated a trail skirting around Highlander Ranch. "Blaine could take this route, which would cut time off the journey."

"Is there more?"

Bay nodded. "There is, Heather." He went on to explain two other properties, the last one long and slender. "It's the farthest property south and runs right into the ranchero they and August purchased from Juan Estrada. It's a lot of land, stretching for miles, and most of it is along the Boundary River." Bay straightened, looking around the table. "I know it seems overwhelming, and it is. Now is the time to move since all the owners are motivated to sell at reasonable prices."

"Ewan and Ian will be sending men to be helping me once the sales are final. The larger ranch has several cowhands." Blaine looked at

Caleb. "I'll be riding there with Bay to meet them this week. He's going to all the properties to finalize the contracts. When I return, I'll be working here until all the deals go through."

Caleb looked at Bay. "How long do you think it will take to close the sales?"

Rubbing the back of his neck, he shrugged. "Hard to say. A month if all goes well and no other investors learn about it. There's always a chance one or more will decide against selling. It's a risk, but Ewan and Ian are determined to buy the land. It's hard to argue with them when the family has the money, the Bank of Conviction is willing to take partial notes on each one, and they have the right person to run them." He glanced at Blaine, his eyes crinkling at the corners.

"Do you plan to leave tomorrow?" Caleb stared at the map, doing his best to memorize the key landmarks.

Blaine glanced at Bay, then shook his head. "There's another matter we have to deal with tomorrow."

"What's that?" Caleb pulled out a chair and sat down.

Blaine considered the question. It had taken a few strong words with Nate, but his friend had finally agreed it was time Caleb and Heather knew what he and Colt were doing. And the name of the man involved.

"Did either of you know Colt is a U.S. Marshal?"

"What?" Heather's mouth gaped open. "The lad told us he guarded gold shipments from the mine."

"He does. The man in charge of the shipments getting to town is Black Jolly."

Caleb slammed his fist on the table. "Son of a..." Pushing away from the table, he stood, placing fisted hands on his hips. "Why didn't Nate say something?"

"Because he's been standing watch on the trail when the trips occur. The lad thought if you knew what was happening, you'd insist on being involved, Caleb."

"And he'd be right."

Geneen walked over to Caleb, placing a hand on his arm. "You've Heather and your ranch to think about. What would happen if you were shot, maybe killed?"

Caleb's face hardened. "I've never run from a fight. Jolly is the man responsible for all the trouble at Circle M. If anyone should be involved, it's me." He sucked in air, letting it out in a frustrated whoosh. "You say you're helping him, Blaine?"

"Aye. Nate, Bay, and I will be watching from points along the trail. Colt believes Black plans to rob the wagon tomorrow, then take off."

Blaine continued, explaining Black's crimes in Texas and how Colt had followed his trail west, learning from Brodie what happened at Circle M.

Heather shook her head. "Black is a busy lad."

Blaine nodded. "And a nasty one, lass."

Caleb crossed his arms, glaring at Blaine. "What time will you be on the trail tomorrow?"

"You aren't joining us, lad."

"You can't stop me, Blaine. I know the trail from the mine to town. It would be easier if you just let me ride along with you rather than me picking a random place on the trail."

Throwing up his hands, Blaine mumbled a curse as he looked at Bay.

"Don't ask me for advice on this one. Caleb's as stubborn as you MacLarens."

Geneen looked between the men, clearing her throat. "I think Heather and I should go along."

"No!" Caleb, Blaine, and Bay all answered.

Crossing her arms, Heather glared at her husband. "And why not? We were there to help you lads when Black came after you."

Caleb stepped next to her, putting an arm around her shoulders, which she shrugged away. "Sweetheart, this is different."

Heather lifted a brow. "Aye? You'll need to be telling me how it's different."

Blaine spoke first. "Colt doesn't know if Black is acting alone or if he has others working for him.

If he has partners, we'd not be knowing how many or where they'll be waiting. It's too dangerous, lass."

Caleb studied his wife's face, knowing how stubborn she could be when it came to not being included with the men. "You and Geneen are needed here. We only did a few chores on Christmas and the work is piling up. We'll be further behind if all of us leave to help Colt."

Bay looked between the women. "Marcus also volunteered. That's five men posted off the trail, plus Colt guarding the wagon."

Heather blew out a frustrated breath, placing her hands on her hips. "Ach. It seems you're right. It's just...I hate to be left behind when my family is in danger."

Drawing her against his chest, Caleb placed a kiss on her forehead. "I'd not be able to focus on the trail if I knew you were there, lass." He lowered his voice so only she could hear. "You've got to think of the wee bairn you're carrying."

She squeezed him once more, then lifted her gaze to his. "Aye, you're right," she whispered. They'd told no one of her suspected pregnancy. Settlers Valley didn't have a doctor, which she and Caleb hoped to change when they rode back to Conviction in a couple weeks to see Doc Tilden to confirm her condition.

Dropping his arms, Caleb stepped away. "It's settled."

Blaine nodded. "Aye. We'll be leaving tomorrow morning at eight. With luck, before the end of the day, Black Jolly will be behind bars and we'll finally be seeing justice."

Nate stared at the ceiling, his thoughts a jumbled mess. He'd returned to the ranch for supper, sitting across from Geneen, who focused her attention on Bay, barely acknowledging him. It seemed getting through to her might not be as easy as he'd hoped.

Geneen's decision to return to the ranch gave him hope she'd consider giving him another chance. After she snubbed him at supper, he wasn't as confident. Giving up on them wasn't in his thoughts. One way or another, he'd make her listen, let her know he'd conquered his demons. It was still a mystery to him how it happened, waking up one morning to realize his mind no longer craved the vile drug.

A soft knock had him swinging his legs off the bed and striding to the door. Opening it, his mouth opened on a surprised breath. She stood before him in her nightdress and wrapper, making it hard to think.

"Geneen."

Licking her lips, she glanced behind him. "I hope I'm not disturbing you."

"Not at all. Is something wrong?" He blocked the doorway, unsure whether to invite her in or step into the hall.

"Yes, and no." Her eyes danced, although he couldn't miss the edge of uncertainty in her voice.

Opening the door wider, he stepped aside. "Do you want to come in?"

She looked up and down the hall before nodding. "For a minute."

Nate nodded to a chair by the window before closing the door, making certain to leave it slightly ajar. Lowering himself to the edge of the bed, he waited for her to start.

Fidgeting with the fabric of her wrapper, she looked around the room so similar to her own. Archie had built several bedrooms, each comparable, yet different. The curtains and bedspread in Nate's room were made of darker colors—burgundies, browns, and greens. It suited him.

"You wanted to talk?"

Pressing her lips together and straightening her shoulders, she looked up. "I need to know if you think there's a chance for us, Nate. If not, you need to tell me." She felt her heart lodge in her throat when he didn't answer. "I understand if you no longer have feelings for me. It's just, well...I need to hear it from you."

Nate had a hard time controlling the incessant pounding in his chest. She'd surprised him with her request. He didn't know what he'd expected, but it wasn't this. Standing, he walked to within a foot of her. Leaning down, he took her hand in his, rubbing his thumb over her palm.

"I'm not sure what to say."

She looked at their joined hands. "The truth would be best."

Sucking in a breath, Nate knelt before her. "I can't see a future for me without you, Geneen. No matter how I've tried to tell myself to let you go, let you find a man without the scars I carry, I can't do it. After what happened before you left for Circle M, I never thought you'd allow me another chance. Is that what you're offering?"

She fought to keep the tears pooling in her eyes from falling before one slipped loose, rolling down her cheek. When Nate dropped her hand to swipe the tear away, she couldn't hold back a sob.

"Yes, it's what I'm offering."

Cupping her face with his hand, he leaned forward, brushing his lips across hers. When she leaned into the kiss, he deepened it, wrapping his arm around her.

Slanting his mouth over hers, he groaned at her ragged sigh. Her lips were warm, soft, allowing him access he'd only dreamed of for the last few months. He wanted to do more, much more, but now wasn't the time.

They needed to start fresh, give themselves a chance to make sure a future was what they both wanted. And he needed to prove to Geneen she could trust him.

Breaking the kiss, he pulled away, his chest squeezing at the glazed look in her eyes. Smiling, he stood, holding out his hand to help her stand.

"I accept your offer, Geneen. Thank you."

Chapter Seventeen

Conviction

"Sheriff!" Ira Greene ran down the boardwalk, doing his best to keep his short legs pumping. Holding up the letter, he yelled again. "Brodie!" This time, he got his attention. Turning around, Brodie walked toward him, watching as the older man fought for breath. "I haven't run so far since I was this big." Ira held his hand about three feet above the boardwalk. "I think what you've been waiting for has come."

Brodie took the letter Ira held out, seeing it came from Settlers Valley. When his gaze moved to the recipient, his breath caught. "This can't be the right one."

"It's the only one, Sheriff. Not much mail between the two towns, but if I recall right, there've been other letters from Settlers Valley to the same person. Isn't she—"

Brodie grabbed his arm, cutting off whatever else Ira planned to say. Ushering him between two buildings, he glanced around. "Don't mention this to anyone."

Ira shook his head, his eyes round as saucers.

Handing the letter back, Brodie's mind worked as he tried to understand the connection

231

between Black Jolly and the person receiving his letters. "When does she come to pick up her mail?"

"She's living at Mrs. Baker's boardinghouse. If there's mail, I usually deliver it on my way home each night."

Brodie thought a moment, looking toward the street. "Stop by the jail and let me know when you're ready to make your delivery tonight. I want to follow you."

Nodding briskly, Ira grinned. "Yes, sir. It'll be right after I close."

"I'll be waiting."

Brodie walked back to the boardwalk and straight to his horse. Swinging into the saddle, he rode the gelding down a couple streets, stopping in front of August Fielder's law office. Dismounting, he spotted Sam not far down the street.

"Sam!"

Spinning on his heels, his deputy and brother-in-law turned around. Taking long strides, he reached Brodie in seconds.

"I've news from Ira."

"The letter came?"

"Aye. Ira says the same person has received other letters from Settlers Valley."

"Who's the letter addressed to?"

Glancing up and down the street, Brodie shook his head. "I'm on my way to talk with August. Come with me."

Strolling inside, Brodie waved to August's assistant as he headed up the stairs to the law offices, ignoring the young man's surprised look. August had a large office on one side of the building while Bay Donahue had a smaller one on the other side. Knocking, Brodie opened the door without waiting for a response, coming to an abrupt stop.

"Aunt Kyla?"

She jumped up from where she sat on the edge of August's desk, her face turning a deep red. He hadn't seen her so gussied up since well before her husband, Angus, passed away.

August stood, glancing at Kyla before coming around the desk. "Brodie. Did we have an appointment?"

Shaking his head, Brodie's gaze moved between the two. "Nae, we didn't."

Letting out a sigh, August motioned Brodie and Sam to chairs around a table. Taking Kyla's hand, he whispered something to her before pulling out a chair for her.

"I'll make this short. I've asked Kyla for permission to court her. She's agreed, but I've yet to speak to her sons. We'd both appreciate it if you'd say nothing until I've talked to Colin and Camden."

Brodie nodded, a slow grin spreading across his face.

"Sam?" August asked.

"This may get me in trouble, but I won't say a word, not even to Jinny."

"Good. Let me walk Kyla outside and I'll be right back up." He slipped her arm through his, escorting her into the hall.

"Aunt Kyla?"

Stopping, she turned to face her nephew. "Aye, Brodie?"

"It's grand news."

She flushed again, smiling in a way he hadn't seen since before his uncle's death.

Sam settled back in his chair, waiting until they disappeared down the stairs. "Well, I'll be."

Brodie nodded. "Aye."

"Did you have any idea Kyla had an interest in him?"

"Not a one. Although, if I think on it, there were times they spent several minutes alone when he'd come to Sunday supper. After Angus, I never thought she'd be interested in another man."

"You know, Brodie, Kyla isn't an old woman. She's still beautiful."

"Aye, she is. It's just...I've not thought of her having an interest in another relationship. It will be taking some getting used to."

"I can just imagine what Colin and Camden will think. It might be a good thing Blaine is already gone."

Brodie chuckled. "Aye. It might be."

"All right, gentlemen." August shut the door behind him, taking a seat at the table. "What brings you to my office?"

"That cannot be. She'd never associate with a man like Black Jolly. She must be receiving letters from someone else in Settlers Valley. Maybe even Heather or Geneen."

Brodie shook his head. "Nae. I doubt either of the lasses would have a reason to write her, especially Heather."

August scrubbed a hand down his face, nodding. "No, probably not. What do you plan to do?"

Brodie glanced out the window, staring at the large, billowing clouds moving south, then looked at August. "Ira will deliver the mail to the boardinghouse tonight. He'll stop by the jail on his way. I plan to go with him."

"Do you plan to speak with her?"

"Aye. There's no other way to discover who the letter is from."

Rubbing his jaw, August nodded. "I should go with you."

"I don't think that's a good idea, sir." Sam looked between Brodie and August. "In my experience, it would be best for Brodie to go alone. You might want to be close by, maybe down at the Gold Dust. I'll wait on the boardwalk and alert you if there's any trouble."

"Surely she wouldn't cause a ruckus," August gasped.

Sam shook his head, leaning forward. "If it is the woman we seek and she's associated with Black, there's no telling what she might do. I'll be a few steps down the street and you'll be close by."

August looked at Brodie. "What do you think?"

"I agree with Sam. If there's no connection, it's best she not think you're aware of me checking on her. She's a nice lass and hasn't been in town long. We don't want to make settling in more difficult for her."

"Then I'll come to the jail and wait with you for Ira. I certainly hope you're wrong and his connection in Conviction isn't her."

"Aye. So do I."

Brodie pulled his pocket watch out and checked the time, glancing across the desk at Sam and August. "Ira should be here any time now."

A few minutes later, the door opened, Ira stepping inside. "I'm heading to the boardinghouse, Sheriff." He nodded at August and Sam.

"We're ready."

Ira's eyes widened. "You aren't all going, are you?"

August took a couple steps toward him. "If you have no objection."

Shaking his head, Ira stuttered. "Uh, no, Mr. Fielder. No objection from me."

Grabbing their hats, they followed Ira outside, crossed the street, and headed toward the boardinghouse. August slipped into the Gold Dust while Sam continued a bit farther before taking a seat in an empty chair. Brodie continued with Ira, stopping outside the boardinghouse.

"You sure about this, Sheriff?"

Brodie nodded. "You go on inside and deliver the mail, then head home. I'll wait until she comes down to collect her mail before I go inside."

Relief flooded Ira's face. "I don't want to get in any trouble for sharing the information with you."

"No one's going to be reporting you, Ira. All you did was tell me a letter arrived from Settlers Valley. Neither of us opened it, so I don't see how you'd get in trouble."

"If you say so." Stepping inside, Ira closed the door. "Mrs. Baker," he called toward the back. "I've got the mail."

Shuffling out from the kitchen, the elderly woman came toward him. "Good evening, Mr. Greene." She took the mail from his hand, looking through it.

"You've got a letter from your daughter, ma'am."

"Yes, I see that. And there's one from my brother." Ignoring the last letter, she looked up. "Thank you for bringing it by. You know, I can walk down the street and pick it up."

"Well now, Mrs. Baker, I've been doing this since before your husband passed. It's on my way home and no bother at all."

"Someday, you and the missus should come by and have supper with us. I'd love the company."

"I appreciate the offer. I'll let the missus know." Touching a finger to the brim of his hat, he nodded. "Well, I'll be on my way now."

"See you next time, Mr. Greene." Holding the mail, she returned to the kitchen.

Stepping outside, Ira looked at Brodie. "I'll be heading home now, Sheriff."

"Thanks, Ira. I appreciate your help."

Brodie leaned against the outside wall of the building, glancing through the front window every few minutes. A good thirty minutes went by before Mrs. Baker walked back out, carrying plates of food to the large dining room table. When she'd brought out everything, she moved to the bottom of the stairs and rang the bell.

Several men and a couple young women came down, each greeting her before heading to their places at the table. Brodie recognized a few, but not all. The woman he wanted to talk to came down last, stopping when Mrs. Baker held out the letter.

When the older woman joined her guests at the table, the young boarder stayed behind, walking into the parlor and tearing open the letter. As she read, her face contorted, taking on a pained expression. Brodie knew he'd never get a better chance than now. Opening the door, he moved toward her.

"Good evening, Miss Harris."

Miranda jumped, turning to face Brodie, a hand at her throat. "Oh, Sheriff. You startled me."

"Apologies, ma'am. Appears you received a letter."

The young schoolteacher looked down, her hands shaking. "Yes."

"From your parents?"

"Um, no."

Brodie watched fear show in her eyes, her breath coming in short bursts. "When I walked inside, you didn't look too well. Hope it isn't bad news."

Her bottom lip trembled, her face losing most of its color. "It's, well...it's not good news." She held the letter to her chest.

"Bad news is never good. You know, I've got relatives up in Settlers Valley. Have you heard of it?"

She shot Brodie a startled look, eyes wide with panic. "Why, yes. It's north of here, isn't it?"

"I'm thinking you already know where it is. Don't you, Miss Harris?"

Closing her eyes, Miranda shook her head slowly. Glancing down at the letter, her body began to shake so much she wrapped her arms around her waist, lowering herself onto the sofa. Rocking back and forth, a small keening sound slipped from her lips.

"I don't know what to do." Her words came out on a quiet sob. The letter in her lap, she placed her hands over her face and wept.

Sitting at the other end of the sofa, Brodie shifted toward her, seeing Sam through the front window. "Are you all right, lass?"

Continuing to rock back and forth, Miranda shook her head. "No, I don't think I am."

"May I see the letter?"

Dropping her hands from her face, she looked at him. The misery Brodie saw ripped through him. Whatever was in the letter, whatever Miranda knew, couldn't be good.

"Miss Harris?"

Glancing at the letter in her lap, she swiped tears off her face. Picking it up, her hands shook as she held it out to Brodie. "He isn't like this."

His brows furrowing, he took it from her hand, unfolding it. As he read, his heart began to pound as anger rushed through him. At the end, there was no signature, only the initials B. J.

"Is this from Black Jolly?"

Nodding, she hiccupped on another sob.

"Is he your husband?"

She continued to stare at her lap, shaking her head.

"Lover?"

Her gaze whipped up to meet his, her face full of shock. "No."

"Then who is he?"

Catching her bottom lip in her teeth, she looked away.

"Miss Harris, this letter is from someone who intends to break the law, maybe even kill people in the process. I believe he's the same man who attacked my family's ranch. He took the time to write you a letter, and I'm guessing it's not the first. Please answer me, lass. Who is he to you?"

Closing her eyes, Miranda tightened her arms around her waist, rocking back and forth once more.

"Miranda. Please, answer me."

Opening eyes filled with misery, she opened her mouth, then closed it. Sucking in a slow breath, Miranda's gaze met his.

"He's my brother."

Chapter Eighteen

Settlers Valley

Josiah Lloyd scribbled the message from Sheriff MacLaren as it came across the wire. He'd barely put his hat on a hook when the notification sounded. Sighing, Josiah took a seat, never imagining the importance of this particular telegram until he wrote it out. Stomach churning, he folded the message, stuffed it into a pocket, and dashed outside toward Dahlia's boardinghouse, shoving the door open and hurrying inside.

"Mrs. Keach, are you here?" Josiah's frantic gaze took in the empty dining room.

"Josiah Lloyd, what on earth are you shouting about?"

"Is Mr. Dye in his room?"

Crossing her arms, she shook her head. "He ate his breakfast and took off without a word. I've never seen a man in such a rush as Mr. Dye."

Biting the inside of his cheek, Josiah considered what to do next. "It's important I find him. Do you know where he went?"

"No, sir, I don't. I don't make it a habit to nose into the affairs of my guests."

Josiah would've laughed if he didn't know the contents of the telegram. The entire town knew Dahlia Keach lived for gossip.

"Have you seen Sheriff Polk this morning?" Josiah looked out the front window, concern lodging in his chest.

"Pfft. That man is as worthless as a tick. I doubt he's even out of bed yet. You know, now that I think on it, Mr. Dye does spend time at the Lucky Lady with Marcus Kamm's helper." Dahlia pursed her lips. "Oh, what is his name?"

"Nate Hollis?"

"Why, yes. That's the man. You might try the livery to see if he knows where Mr. Dye is."

"I'll do that, Mrs. Keach. If you see Mr. Dye, please tell him I have a telegram for him."

Josiah hurried along the boardwalk, coming to a stop when he saw the doors of the blacksmith shop closed and chained. Moving to the livery in back, he peered over the fence, seeing no activity. He rubbed his forehead, confounded on what to do next.

Reaching into his pocket, he removed the message, reading it once more. As urgent as it seemed, he'd done all he could. He thought of rousing the sheriff, but dismissed the idea with a quick shake of his head. As Dahlia implied, the man wouldn't give a whit about what another sheriff warned. He'd most likely crumple up the paper and toss it into the stove.

Looking up and down the street once more, Josiah slipped the message back into his pocket. Delivery would have to wait until Colt showed up.

Highlander Ranch

Geneen and Heather worked well as a team, rounding up strays, merging them with the main herd. They stayed alert for any danger, their movements fluid as they performed the chores both understood well. This morning, their minds were elsewhere.

Rounding up three more head from an obscure gulch, Geneen reined up Gypsy. Heather sat atop Shamrock no more than five yards away, her gaze fixed on the western hills—the direction of the mine. Looking up, Geneen gauged the time to be after nine.

"The lads will be in position now."

Geneen's throat constricted on Heather's words. "Yes, I suppose so." Her grip tightened on the reins.

"I'll not know a moment's peace until Caleb and the others are back."

"They'll be coming home, Heather. They've been through this before. We all have. Today isn't a day for them to die." Geneen wished she felt as confident as her words indicated. She'd slept little, her mind on Nate and their shared time in his room.

She wished he'd allowed her to stay the night, but it wasn't to be. His sense of propriety and respect for her wouldn't allow it, and Geneen couldn't fault him for it. They had a lot of mending to do, and she meant to do her best to see them succeed.

"Caleb and I plan a quick trip to Conviction in a few weeks."

Geneen realized she'd been lost in her own thoughts, not noticing Heather move to within a few feet of her. "Do you mean to Circle M?"

"Nae. Not until we see Doc Tilden."

Geneen's features shifted to alarm. "Are you or Caleb ill?"

"Nae. Well, I've not been feeling sick. At least not yet." Heather rested a hand on her stomach.

Her eyes widening, Geneen's mouth gaped open. "You're with child?"

Grinning, Heather nodded. "Aye. At least the signs are there, the same as they were with Sarah. I told Caleb there's no reason to make the trip to Conviction since we'll be moving the cattle in a few months." She looked down at her still flat stomach. "You know how the lad is. He's saying we can't wait that long to see a doctor."

"Women do it all the time."

"Aye, they do. And most out this way never see a doctor. Caleb doesn't care what most women do. He's determined to have Doc Tilden examine me. I'm thinking what he truly wants is to talk the doctor into moving to Settlers Valley. I've told him the lad won't be moving when he's only been in Conviction a short time."

Geneen shook her head. "Probably not, but he may know of someone looking for a place out here."

"Aye, I'm hoping that's true. So, what I'm really wanting to ask is if you'd be all right watching the ranch while we're gone? Caleb's thinking we'll be gone three days. The family will be having fits if we don't stay at Circle M at least one night."

"Visit with them as long as you want, Heather. I'll be fine here. Besides, Blaine said it should take less than four days for him and Bay to visit the properties. He'll be here to help out."

"And Nate."

Biting her lower lip, Geneen nodded. "Maybe. He's got his job in town, but I'm certain he'll do what he can."

"I saw you and the lad before he left with Caleb, Blaine, and Bay. Seems you've been making progress."

Geneen felt her face flush at the reminder of how Nate kissed her before leaving. The intimacy in front of the family and Bay surprised her.

She shrugged, not willing to rely too much on what had been said the night before. "We've agreed to try again."

"That's good news, lass. I've not had a chance to tell you, but the lad's been doing better. He's much like the man he was before the opium took control." Heather grimaced. "It's a nasty business. I'm hopeful it will be staying out of Settlers Valley."

Geneen hoped so as well.

A fierce wind blew as the miners loaded the wagon. Colt tugged on the collar of his coat, keeping his gaze locked on Black, who sat atop his large stallion, looking bored with the activities. Something about the way his eyes flickered told Colt the man wasn't as relaxed as he appeared.

The same driver as always sat on the bench, lines secured beside him. The other guard, an average looking, slightly overweight younger man, smoked a cheroot a few feet from Colt. He seemed a good sort, jovial and easy-going. Colt knew looks could be misleading.

Before the first load, Colt and Nate discussed the best place to attack the wagon, deciding the middle of the route seemed best. The trail veered away from the Feather River through thick trees, dense shrub, and thick rock formations. After less than half a mile, the trail changed, moving through open land within yards of the river. It offered everything an outlaw would want, including side trails going east. Easy escapes from the main road.

Shifting in the saddle, Colt stared down the trail. By now, Nate and the others would be in position, their guns ready. If Black made his move today, Colt had no doubt who would come out on top.

Nate huddled down in the usual spot, his back pressed against a large rock. Caleb hid across the trail, while Blaine took a position several yards south. Marcus and Bay preferred to be north of the others, with clear views of the trail as it turned into the dense growth.

A bird call Nate had heard many times wafted across the trail, forcing a smile. Caleb and Blaine were communicating. Back in their homeland of Scotland, the MacLarens had devised an uncomplicated, yet effective way of sending messages. Their great-grandfathers had passed it to the sons, and so it went until all the men and women at Circle M knew what each sound meant.

Geneen spent countless hours teaching Nate, laughing as he tried to mimic her and the others. Over time, his skills improved enough he recognized Blaine and Caleb communicating about the open trail to the south. He immediately recognized their mistake. They should've taken positions to the north, where Bay and Marcus waited.

Shaking his head, Nate snorted. "Hindsight," he mumbled to himself as he drew his six-shooter from its holster, checking the cylinder one more time. Alongside him lay his rifle. It had taken a long time to adjust to bracing it on his left shoulder instead of his right. He'd persevered, determined not to let the loss of the lower half of his left arm stop him from a normal life. He now felt as proficient with the weapon as he had before the war.

Pulling out his pocket watch, Nate checked the time. All his instincts told him Black would go for the gold today. By tonight, the outlaw would be in jail or dead.

"Roll out." Black's order spurred the driver into action.

Slapping the lines, he guided the animals south, along the trail to Settlers Valley. With today's heavy load, Colt knew it would take longer than the previous trips. Pushing his hat back, he lifted his face to a rapidly darkening sky. The wind no longer whipped around them, but the weather was changing from the clear sky of early morning.

They'd been on the trail ten minutes when rain pelted them in persistent waves, soaking them through. Colt saw Black ride to the side of the wagon, leaning toward the driver.

"Take the trail up ahead."

The driver shook his head. "It's gonna be a tough one with the load we've got. The rain ain't gonna hurt nothing."

Pulling his gun, Black pointed it at the driver's head. "Take the trail."

Colt had seen the narrow path before, never thinking it wide enough for the overloaded wagon. According to the driver, it would be a hard ride. Worse, Colt didn't know where it reentered the main trail.

Cursing himself for not scouting alternate routes before today, he followed behind the wagon, unable to do anything else.

The trail proved to be all the driver feared. Narrowing in places so the wagon barely fit, riddled with ruts high enough to break the axel. The one positive aspect being the tall, dense canopy, which kept the rain from reaching them.

Even with the cover overhead, rain began to soak the trail, creating low patches of thick mud. The wagon stopped twice, requiring Colt and the other guard to dismount while Black watched them dislodge the wheels.

By some miracle Colt didn't dwell on, the wagon made it through, merging back with the main trail. Breathing a sigh of relief, he looked around, realizing they were still a little north of where Nate and the others were waiting.

Another ten minutes passed in quiet as the rain let up and the sky cleared. He knew they'd passed the locations where Bay and Marcus waited. Caleb and Nate would be next, with Blaine at the southern tip of the trail where they felt certain Black would make his move.

Colt began to wonder if his instincts had failed him when a shot rang out. Drawing his gun, he reined his horse in a circle, surprised to see two men ride up. Both wore handkerchiefs over their faces, their bodies hidden behind black greatcoats, guns aimed at the guards.

"No one move and you'll make it through this alive." The smaller of the two rode toward Colt.

"Drop your gun and remove the rifle from the scabbard."

A part of him wanted to refuse, raise his gun and see what would happen. Colt knew it would be a fool's action, considering his own men were perched above the outlaws with perfect views of the trail. He did as the outlaw ordered, dropping his weapons to he ground.

"Slowly now," the outlaw cautioned, waving his gun for Colt to continue while Black sat on the other side of the wagon, a sneer stretched across his face.

Colt stilled at the sound of another shot. Whipping his head to the side, he saw the young guard clutch his chest, the larger of the two outlaws chuckling.

"Thought I saw the fella move for his gun."

Colt knew that voice. Before he could react, a series of shots sounded from the rocks around them. Slipping to the ground, he grabbed the gun he'd dropped on the ground. The smaller guard lay unmoving a few feet away.

Colt scooted into the bushes, searching for cover, as Black and the other outlaw swung their horses in a circle.

"Let's get out of here." The outlaw shot in wild succession, hitting the driver, unable to find the target he sought.

More shots rang out, barely missing both men. Colt aimed his gun at Black just before the man jumped from his horse and onto the back of the wagon. "I'm not leaving without the gold."

"You're a fool."

Without warning, Black leveled his gun at his comrade and fired. "I said I'm not leaving without the gold."

Colt watched, fascinated at what he saw. Black whistled for his horse, then leaned over the wagon to grab his saddlebags. Ignoring the danger surrounding him, he began stuffing gold into the pouches.

Behind him, Colt heard his friends approach. In front of him, Bay and Marcus walked toward the wagon, guns drawn, as fascinated as Colt at Black's actions.

Surrounding the wagon, their aim never wavering from the outlaw, the six men stopped.

"It's over, Jolly. Get down from the wagon." Colt moved closer.

"I'm not leaving without this gold." Black glanced up long enough for the others to see the wild glare in his eyes.

Nate took a couple steps closer. "If you don't get down, you'll not get out of this alive."

Black leaned down as if to pick up more gold. Instead, his hand slipped into his boot.

"Don't do it," Nate warned, his aim steady.

In no more than a second, Black pulled the Derringer from his boot. Before he could get the shot off, Nate fired, as did Blaine, the bullets piercing Black's chest. Staggering back, he tripped on the load, raising his arm for one more shot. He never pulled the trigger before another bullet hit him near his heart.

Looking beside him, Nate saw Bay slam his smoking gun back into its holster, a grim smile on his face.

A few moments passed where no one moved. Even the air seemed to still as smoke hung around them.

"The boy's alive." Marcus hovered over the other guard, a hand pushing on the open wound. "We need to get him into town."

Caleb jumped onto the wagon. "The driver's dead."

"Better check the other one." Nate moved past Bay toward the other outlaw. The man lay on his stomach, his arms stretched out on both sides.

"We'd best see who it is." Blaine stood next to him, bending to help Nate roll the body over. Pulling down the handkerchief, Blaine shook his head. "Do you know the man?"

Nate and Colt glanced at each other before Nate spoke. "That's Polk."

Caleb jumped from the wagon, moving beside them, his mouth twisting in disdain. "The sheriff."

Marcus looked toward them, keeping pressure on the guard's wound. "I always knew the man was a crook. Never thought he'd be involved with something like this, though."

"What now?" Bay asked.

Colt looked around, a hint of grim satisfaction on his face. "Load the guard and the bodies. We've got a load of gold to deliver."

Chapter Nineteen

"I've done all I can." Dahlia checked the bandage once more, then pulled a blanket under the guard's chin. "The rest is up to God."

Colt stared at the unconscious young man who he insisted be placed in his bed at the boardinghouse. "Where'd you learn to patch up a gunshot wound?"

Gathering her supplies, Dahlia offered him a patient look. "My father was a doctor. I often assisted him, even after he hired a nurse." She chuckled. "He told me the patients liked the way I took care of them."

"The town is lucky to have you, Mrs. Keach."

"What we need is a real doctor, Mr. Dye. One knowledgeable about fevers, tuberculosis, and childbirth. I've tried sending our needs to doctors in Sacramento and San Francisco, without any success. Most don't want to give up their patients and uproot their families for the unknown of what they consider a wild, frontier town." She looked down at the young man with the bandaged shoulder. "After today, I can't say as I blame them."

"Seems you're going to need a new sheriff as well."

"Not to say a bad word about the dead, but Polk wasn't a good man. I never could abide him and his ways." Picking up her tray of supplies, she turned toward the door. "It's a surprise he partnered with that outlaw, though. What a retched pair they would've made."

After Dahlia closed the door, Colt pulled up a chair, taking a seat to watch the patient. They'd been on several runs together, introduced themselves. Staring, he felt a pang of guilt. He couldn't remember the man's name. *Joe, Billy, Henry.* Colt pinched the bridge of his nose as he tried to remember.

The door opened. "How's he doing?" Nate walked in, studying the man lying in bed.

"He'll be all right if infection doesn't start."

"You never mentioned his name."

Colt rubbed his brow. "George. George Howell." He didn't know how he remembered, but was glad he did.

"Must not be more than nineteen."

Colt nodded. "If that. I do hope he pulls through."

"We took the bodies to the undertaker. The sheriff has no family. No one knows the other outlaw. And Black? Who knows if the man has kin or not."

"This came for you, Mr. Dye." Dahlia walked into the room, holding out a telegram. She bent over George, looking at the bandage, then straightened. "We'll know if he's going to make it in another couple days."

Opening the message, Colt's brows rose. "Brodie found the woman Black wrote to in Conviction. Miranda Harris. Do you know her?"

"Miranda Harris?" Nate shook his head. "I can't say as I do. She might've arrived in town after I left."

"Seems she and Black are connected. She's his sister."

Nate shook his head. "Did she know about all he's done?"

Colt skimmed the message again. "He didn't say. Brodie warned us of the robbery. Said Black had a partner." He set the telegram down. "This might've gotten to us late, but he had the information right."

"I'll ask Geneen if she knows anything about Miss Harris. Do you plan to take Black's body back to Conviction?"

"I wasn't planning on it. Now that I know he has a sister, I'll be taking him there tomorrow." Colt leaned forward, resting his arms on his legs. "Any message you want me to pass on to Brodie?"

His jaw working, Nate shook his head. "Not now. I've got unfinished business here." Rubbing the stubble on his chin, he looked at Colt. "Have you ever considered getting out of the Marshals Service and doing something else?"

Leaning back in the chair, he shrugged. "I'm a lawman, Nate. This is one of the best jobs in the country. There'd have to be a real good reason for me to make a change."

Nate thought of Geneen. He'd do anything for her, including changing jobs or moving cross-country. "Do you have a woman waiting for you someplace?"

Chuckling, Colt shook his head. "A relationship is pretty hard to keep with this job. Now, if I were a shopkeeper, rancher, or professional man like Bay, settled in one town, it might be possible. Nah. It's not in the future for me."

"What about a sheriff? Settlers Valley needs a new one."

Colt rubbed the back of his neck. "If I ever considered a sheriff or deputy job, it would have to be in a town larger than here. I need a little more action."

Nate's thinking tended to be the opposite. Since coming to Settlers Valley, he found a peace elusive to him since before the war. The family ranch offered hard work, but a satisfaction he'd lost since moving west. With Geneen back at Caleb's, he had no desire to leave.

"You, though, would be the perfect man to replace Polk."

"Me?" Nate snorted. "I have a job with Marcus."

"He'd support you."

Nate raised a brow. "How would you know?"

A rueful grin tilted the corners of Colt's mouth. "He mentioned it to me. Marcus thinks you'd be a great choice. He's going to speak to a few people about it."

Crossing his arms, he planted his feet shoulder width apart. "Don't you think he should be speaking to me first?"

"Nope. I believe he has the right idea. You're planning to stay here a while, you have the skills, and you're one of the most honest men I know. There's no one else I've seen who can come close to you." Colt shook his head, enjoying Nate's befuddled expression. "Think about it, Nate. It could be the perfect solution for you."

Highlander Ranch

"Do you plan to head out tomorrow, Bay?" Geneen handed him a bowl of potatoes. Tonight, Nate sat on her left, his thigh resting against hers, her pulse spiking each time he moved.

"Blaine and I will both be riding out soon after dawn. With luck, we'll visit the properties and be back within two days. Three at most."

"I'm thinking you're excited to see what the family will be buying, Blaine."

He looked at Heather, a slow grin spreading across his face. "Aye. I never expected Ewan and Ian to trust me with such a challenge."

"I'm not knowing why not. You're the perfect choice. With your da gone, Kyla needs Colin and Sarah with her. Quinn and Emma won't leave with her family's ranch a mile away. Brodie's the sheriff. Plus, he and Maggie are expecting a baby within a few months. You're single, with no commitments, and you're as good a rancher as any of us, with a good mind for business."

Blaine offered a distracted nod. When she'd spoken of no ties, his mind formed an image of Lia, feeling an odd tug on his heart. He'd never felt such a connection with another woman. Too bad her life was in Conviction while his would now be in Settlers Valley.

"I'll be needing to find men. Ewan and Ian will be sending a few once the land is transferred into the MacLaren name, but I'm thinking more will be needed."

Nate swallowed his stew, leaning forward. "Colt is taking Black's body back to Conviction tomorrow. He could talk to Brodie about spreading the word."

Caleb's fork stopped midway to his mouth. "Why would he take the body back there?"

"Seems Black's sister is Miranda Harris."

"Miranda?" Caleb's fork dropped to his plate. "That's not possible."

"You know her?" Nate asked.

"A little," Caleb mumbled.

"Miranda would've liked to have been knowing Caleb much better."

Bay cocked his head at Heather while Blaine chuckled.

"Heather..." Caleb cautioned.

"Ach, lad. You know the lass liked you."

"I liked her, too. Still do. But I wanted another woman." He leaned over, placing a kiss on her cheek, then looked at Nate, his expression sobering. "You're certain she's Black's sister?"

He nodded. "Brodie sent Colt a telegram. Miranda confirmed it."

"Does she know all he's done?" Geneen looked at Nate.

He shook his head. "Brodie didn't mention anything in the telegram."

Bay leaned back in his chair, crossing his arms. "I hope she doesn't. It won't end well for her if she knew of his exploits."

Blaine steepled his fingers under his chin. "If she is arrested, would August defend her?"

Bay thought a moment, then nodded. "I believe he would. He has strong connections to her family. It's interesting he never mentioned a brother."

"He may not have known," Geneen whispered as she shoved her plate away.

Reaching over, Nate covered her hand with his, squeezing. "At least it's over for Black. He'll no longer be a threat to anyone."

Bay cleared his throat. "I hear there's other news. Much more pleasant than what we've been discussing."

"What news, lad?" Heather asked.

"Before we rode back this afternoon, Marcus said he'd already spoken to several people. It appears a number of them want Nate to take over as sheriff."

Heather clapped her hands together. "It's a grand idea."

Caleb nodded. "I agree." He looked at Nate. "You've the experience and people in town trust you."

Blaine's gaze narrowed. "Have you decided to stay in Settlers Valley, lad?"

Geneen looked over at him, sucking in a slow breath as her heart pounded. She'd been wondering the same. They had so little time together since she returned, there'd been no opportunity to ask.

Without looking at Geneen, Nate shrugged. "I've been thinking of staying."

Caleb glanced between Nate and Geneen. "If you became sheriff, you could remain here at the ranch."

"*If*, Caleb. I've not been offered the job, and with all the work Marcus has right now, it would be hard to leave him."

Heather's face lit up. "You could be sheriff and still be helping Marcus. From what I've been hearing, and in spite of Black's actions, not much seems to go on in Settlers Valley. Polk didn't even have a deputy."

Blaine nodded. "I'm thinking Heather has a good idea, lad. Take over for Polk and work for Marcus when he needs you."

Clearing her throat, Geneen's gaze moved around the table. "Maybe, well...Nate may not want to stay here." She slipped her hand out from under his. "He might want to return to Conviction. Brodie would take him back, or he could work at Circle M." She refused to look at Nate as she spoke, afraid she'd see he agreed.

When he didn't correct her, Geneen felt all the hope of the night before flee.

Heather pushed from the table and stood. "I'll be getting dessert now."

"If you don't mind, Geneen and I would like to walk outside for a while." Standing, he held out his hand.

"Nae. You take as long as you want. I'll leave some for both of you in the kitchen...if the lads don't eat it all."

Catching her lower lip between her teeth, Geneen grasped his hand, noticing he didn't let go until they reached the front door. Slipping into their coats, Nate grabbed her hand again before walking outside. He took a path around the corrals toward the Feather River, knowing his destination. Pushing through the dense growth, he rounded a corner, slowing his pace, grateful for the clear sky and almost full moon. The fallen log lay a few feet from the edge of the river, making it the perfect spot for them to talk.

"We're here."

Geneen looked around, her gaze moving across the rippling water. "It's lovely here."

"I thought you'd like it." Lowering himself onto the log, he drew her down next to him.

"However did you find it?"

He chuckled. "It wasn't hard. I took off one night after supper, before going to Archie's house, and ended up here. The trick was finding my way back." Letting go of her hand, he settled his arm around her shoulders. "I've already told you about my family's place near Harrisburg."

"Yes. It sounds beautiful."

"It is. The Susquehanna River borders our property. Each year it brought greener pastures and more water than we could ever use. This place reminds me of what I left behind."

Her heart pounded, dread building as she guessed what he wanted to tell her. "Is that why you brought me here? To let me know you've decided to return to Pennsylvania?"

Pulling her closer to him, Nate kissed her forehead. "Yes, and no. One day, I do want to return to visit my family."

"You don't plan to stay?" She hated the way her voice broke on the last.

"No, Geneen. I have no plans to stay. I've always loved working with horses, but unlike my father, I'm not a breeder. After living out here where you can ride for miles without seeing a soul, the crowded cities of the east no longer appeal to me. There must be close to twenty thousand people in Harrisburg by now."

"Caleb said he thinks there are less than three hundred in Settlers Valley. It would be a change."

"I'm thinking a visit would be enough. Maybe this summer so I could help Pa tend the crops and work the horses."

She turned to look up into his face. "What if Bay is right and the town offers you the job as sheriff?"

Nate stared at the river, relaxing at the way the moonlight played over the water. "I don't know. I'm not certain now is the time."

"In my opinion, you'd make a wonderful sheriff. I truly believe you'd succeed at anything you tried."

He threw back his head and laughed.

Shoving lightly on his chest, Geneen pulled away. "Don't laugh. You're a gifted man with many talents, including the ability to make the most of what life gave you. Do you know how many would've given up or settled for less than what they could achieve after losing an arm?"

His eyes gleamed at her faith in him. Geneen had always had more faith in him than he had in himself.

"No. Do you?"

Twisting her mouth into a grimace, she shook her head. "Well, no. I do recall Ewan once saying he heard there were hundreds of men who'd lost legs or arms who now beg on the streets back east. Did you ever once consider it a choice?"

Drawing in a breath, he acknowledged in brief moments of deep despair, he'd wondered if he'd ever reach the point where begging was the only way to put food in his stomach. He'd never allowed himself to dwell on those moments. Too many men suffered much more than him.

"You must remember, Geneen, there are many with much more grave injuries than mine. Men who lost both arms or an arm and leg. It's no disgrace to beg when you can't find work and are starving."

"No, it isn't. What I'm trying to say is you've made so much more of your life than many others. If they ask you to be the next sheriff, I've no doubt you'd do a fine job." Leaning against his chest, she wrapped her arms around his waist. "If that's what you want."

Resting his chin on the top of her head, he thought of what she said. Nate wavered, but not for lack of confidence in himself. His concerns centered on Marcus. The man had been more than generous, giving him a chance when others had turned their backs.

Nate also loved being a lawman. He felt he'd been born to the job, preparing himself for the good he could do after the war. Letting out a breath, he lifted her onto his lap.

"A decision won't be made tonight. First, we'll see if it's what the town wants. Then I'll have some hard thinking to do." Looking into her upturned face, his breath caught at the love in her eyes. He wondered how he'd ever ridden away from her, thinking they had no chance for a life together.

Now it was all he wanted.

Chapter Twenty

Conviction

"So that's the man who caused so much trouble on the Circle M." Sam Covington stared down at the lifeless form of Black Jolly. "I was hoping he'd make it back here for trial."

Colt continued to hold the tarp so Brodie, Sam, and the other deputies could get a good look at the man who'd wreaked so much destruction on the MacLarens. Waiting until they turned away, he lowered the cover.

"Something snapped at the end. Black might've been half-crazed already, but when we shouted for him to give up, he pulled a Derringer from his boot. We had no choice but to shoot."

Sam clasped him on the shoulder. "You did what you had to do, Colt."

"What of his sister? I brought the body back thinking she'd want to make arrangements."

Brodie crossed his arms. "Miranda Harris hasn't said much since talking to me the night the lass received her brother's letter. She kept insisting the man killing folks wasn't the person she knew growing up."

Colt followed Brodie's gaze up the street to where the schoolhouse stood. "I heard she's a teacher."

"Aye. From what I've been hearing, a good one."

As the other deputies dispersed to make their rounds, Sam moved next to Colt and Brodie. "The question is if Miranda knew of Black's dealings and chose not to warn anyone."

"I spoke to the lass yesterday as she left the schoolhouse. Miranda swears she knew nothing of what he'd done on Circle M. She did apologize, though."

Colt's brow quirked upward. "For what?"

"The lass believes she might have told Black things about the family he later used against us."

Sam tilted his head. "How would she know anything of interest to Black?"

Brodie gave a derisive sound. "She attended a few Sunday suppers at the ranch. You know how the family talks openly about where cattle are located, where we'll be moving them and when. Miranda said Black asked questions about the MacLarens. She never suspected he'd use the information against us."

"Do you believe her?"

Brodie nodded. "Aye, Colt. I do. I don't believe the lass is evil like her brother. He'd cut all ties with everyone in his family, except her. She said most people didn't know her parents had a son. Miranda was young when he left, but she never forgot him. They reunited when she accepted the teaching job here."

"I wonder how he found out she came to Conviction?"

"Another mystery, Sam. I'm thinking it doesn't matter now. The lass is grieving and has a brother to bury. I've no one to prove her story false, so it's best to let her move on with her life."

Colt drew his gaze away from the school. "You're the sheriff, Brodie. You know better than most what's best for the town."

An inscrutable expression crossed Brodie's face. "All I'm knowing is the lass doesn't seem to be a danger to anyone. She had the misfortune of having a brother who went bad." He looked at Colt. "Will you be riding back to Texas?"

"Not yet. I've got to return the wagon to Marcus in Settlers Valley, then I may take a couple weeks off. I already sent a telegram to my superiors and am clear for a spell." He touched the long hair pulled into a queue at the back of his neck. "I might consider getting a shave and haircut."

Brodie pointed. "Right there is the best barber in town."

Sam smirked. "He's the *only* barber in town."

"Aye, Sam, but he does a good job, and Colt does appear to be needing his help."

Chuckling, Colt grabbed his rifle from the wagon. "I'll leave the body with you while I get myself cleaned up. You can find me at the Gold Dust if you have more questions." He took a step, then turned. "Your family is quite remarkable, Brodie."

Watching Colt continue down the street, Brodie felt a wave of pride surge through his body. "Aye, they are," he whispered before climbing onto the wagon.

Highlander Ranch

"Good evening, ladies. The boys and I were wondering if you'd be the Stewarts."

Geneen and Heather straightened, setting down the shovels they used to muck the barn. Their gazes wandered over the three young men, one standing several feet in front of the others.

"I'm Mrs. Stewart and this is Miss MacGregor. What would you be wanting with us?" She studied them, their smooth faces making them appear to be no more than fourteen. The way they stood, cocky and ready for action, plus the sneer on their faces, said they weren't the cherubs they appeared.

273

"We've been riding the countryside, offering deals from a group of well-placed men in San Francisco. They're offering top dollar if you're interested in selling your ranch."

Bay's words of caution came rushing back. She inched closer to the rifle leaning against a stall. "A group of well-placed men, you say?"

"That's right. A partnership to buy land in this area. We've been speaking to a number of ranchers who have an interest in selling. One of them gave us Archie Galloway's name. Said he'd sold his place to the Stewarts."

She glanced at Geneen, who'd moved to within easy reach of her own rifle. Her face showed the same distrust as Heather felt.

"Then you'd be knowing we've had the ranch a short time. I'll be assuring you, my husband and I have no interest in selling."

He took several steps forward, on the edge of crowding Heather against a stall. "Perhaps he'll think different when he hears the terms."

Reaching out, she grabbed the rifle, lifting it enough so he couldn't miss her intentions. "You'd be welcome to speak with Caleb when he returns. You'll be wasting your time, though."

Settling his hand on the butt of his gun, he slowly pulled it out of the holster.

Geneen picked up her rifle, leveling it at the man who made a show of checking the cylinder of his six-shooter before lowering it to his side.

The leader gave the women a cocky sneer. "I've found it's always best to talk before doing something foolish." Sliding the gun back into the holster, he touched the brim of his hat. "Me and the boys will be back. Tell your husband to be ready to talk."

The women didn't lower their guns until the three intruders mounted their horses and rode off. Inhaling a deep breath, Geneen walked to the door of the barn, confirming they'd left the ranch, then turned back to Heather.

"They threatened us."

Heather set down her rifle, settling a hand on her stomach. "Aye, they did. Caleb isn't going to be liking what happened."

"No, he isn't. I'm thinking those men must work for the investors Bay mentioned."

"Who were those men riding out?" Caleb led his horse into the barn, his features strained.

Heather and Geneen explained while Caleb removed Jupiter's tack, the muscles in his jaw flexing.

Heather placed a hand on his arm. "Are you thinking the investors Bay mentioned heard of what Ewan and Ian are doing and sent those men here to make counteroffers?"

Caleb massaged the back of his neck. "From what you've said, I'm thinking they were sent out here to intimidate the ranchers to sell. I also believe they don't know you're a MacLaren or they wouldn't have been so bold."

"So you're believing they'll be back."

He settled an arm around his wife. "Yes, I do. This time, we'll be ready for them."

"I don't like it, Caleb. Those men threatened our women." Nate tossed back the whiskey as the two sat in the office after supper. He'd grown livid at the story Geneen and Heather told, shuddering at the prospect of either of them being hurt.

Caleb hid his grin at Nate's words. He wondered if his friend realized what he'd said.

"I'll ride into town early tomorrow to let Marcus know I'll be staying at the ranch until those men have given up and ridden out."

Caleb held up his hand. "No need for that, Nate. The women and I will be out all day tomorrow rounding up strays and moving them to another pasture. We'll not be back until a little before supper. My guess is those men are staying somewhere in town. I'd rather have you ask around, see if you can find where they are and if anyone knows them."

Nate rubbed his temple to stem the pounding in his head. It started not long after Geneen and Heather related the story of the three men. "You're right. Someone knows where they're staying. I'll ask Mrs. Keach first."

Chuckling, Caleb topped off his drink, tilting the bottle toward Nate, who declined. "Colt says she's up on all the activities in town."

"He tells me the woman misses nothing. She did a real good job stitching up the other guard. Says her father was a doctor back east."

Caleb rubbed his chin. "I wonder if she's a midwife."

Nate's eyes widened. "Is Heather pregnant?"

Looking over the rim of his glass, Caleb grinned. "Seems so. We plan to ride to Conviction in a few weeks to have Doc Tilden look her over."

"Congratulations!" Nate lifted his empty glass in salute.

Caleb's features sobered. "Now I know how Colin felt, worrying so much about Sarah when she was pregnant with Grant."

"If it's all right with you, I'll ask Mrs. Keach if she's ever delivered a baby. It might ease your mind to know there's someone in town who can help when the time comes."

"Maybe it would be best to wait until we return from Conviction. Once Mrs. Keach knows, so will the entire town. I doubt Heather would like that too much."

"What wouldn't I be liking?" She walked through the open door carrying a tray of coffee.

Caleb winced. He hadn't told Heather he planned to let Nate know about the pregnancy. He also wanted to let Blaine and Bay know when they returned from their trip.

"I mentioned the pregnancy to Nate. Hope you don't mind, sweetheart."

Setting the tray down, she saw Geneen leaning against the doorframe. "Ach. I told Geneen, too. I've no doubt I'm carrying a bairn in here." She patted her stomach, then looked at Nate. "He probably told you he wants to ride to Conviction to see Doc Tilden."

Nate didn't have a chance to reply before she continued.

"I'm thinking it's not necessary. A woman knows when she's pregnant. Right, Geneen?"

Feeling her face flush, she bit her lip. "Well, I don't know for a fact. Sarah never had a doubt, and Maggie was pretty certain before she went to see Doc Vickery."

Nate watched her face turn from creamy ivory to slight splotches of red, a sure sign of her discomfort. Standing, he strode toward her, extending his hand.

"How about another walk?"

When she threaded her fingers through his, he looked at Caleb and Heather. "We won't be gone long."

"Take your time," Heather called after them.

Nate took a different path this time, heading between the two houses.

"Archie still has a light burning. I wonder why he never wants to join us for supper."

"I don't know, darlin'." Nate noticed the drawn curtains in the living room. "When I lived with him, Archie said he preferred his own cooking." He chuckled. "I can't recall a time we didn't eat beans, bacon, and biscuits."

Continuing on the path, he felt the warmth from Geneen's hand seep into his, tempering the anger he'd felt at learning about the three men. Intimidation never worked on him, nor had it done more than anger the women. Still, they were vulnerable, and everyone knew it.

"Where are we going?"

"There's a pond up this way. There won't be much going on tonight, but in the early mornings, ducks swim around with their ducklings. We'll have to come back some morning so you can see. Ah, there it is."

She followed his gaze, seeing a crumbling old shack, the roof partially gone, the front door hanging off the hinges. Trees and shrubs created a dense cover, making it almost impossible to see.

"Archie told me about this place. He built it in three days so he and his bride would have a place to live while the bigger house was being constructed." Stepping over the threshold, he kept hold of her hand as he ventured inside. "One big room with a stove and a place for cooking."

Letting go of his hand, she turned in a circle, taking in every detail. "It's wonderful."

Nate laughed. "Only you would see the beauty in a crumbling old shack."

"No. Think about it. This was their beginning, a place they shared dreams of their future and planned the ranch. So much must have been said in this room." She moved to a dilapidated counter, her hand moving over the surface. "I wonder if she learned to cook right here. If Archie perfected his beans, bacon, and biscuits on this very counter."

So caught up in her musings, she didn't hear Nate step behind her until his right arm wrapped around her, drawing Geneen against his chest. Lowering his head, he kissed the tender spot behind her ear, feeling her shiver through the thick coat.

Turning her to face him, he captured her mouth with his, exploring and caressing as his hand moved over her back. He felt her fingers work the buttons on his coat, opening it so her hands could splay across his shirt.

His mouth covered hers, a hungry passion possessing them both, causing waves of heat to course through her. His lips moved across her jaw, down her neck, to the pulsing hollow at the base of her throat. Feeling her tremble, his lips moved back up to take her mouth in a kiss full of all the desire he could no longer contain.

Wrapping her arms around his neck, she drew him down, surprised at her own eager response. She rubbed her body against his, unable to get close enough, incapable of understanding the exploding passion between them.

A low whimper escaped her lips, her eyes widening in surprise as he drew away on a rough growl, resting his forehead against hers. Mouth still stinging from his kisses, she tried to control her ragged breathing. Her body ached with need, a need she had no idea how to fulfill.

Stepping away, Nate closed his coat, leaning down to place a soft kiss on the tip of her nose. He longed to say the words lodged in his throat.

"I love you, Nate."

His chest tightened on the confession. Lifting his hand, he tucked a strand of hair behind her ear. "I love you, too, Geneen."

Her slow smile caused his heart to swell. Returning her smile, he wrapped his arms around her, drawing her against him. "We need to get back, sweetheart. Being alone with you is proving to be more of a challenge than I can handle."

"You seem to have no problem handling me at all, Mr. Hollis."

Chuckling, he gave her one last squeeze. "Ah, Geneen, you are going to be the death of me."

Chapter Twenty-One

"Three committed to selling on the terms agreed to with Ewan and Ian." Bay paced Caleb's office, too agitated to sit down. "I'll be completing the contracts while I'm here so we can get their signatures." Placing fisted hands on his hips, he glared at no one in particular. "I don't understand the hesitation by the others. They've been made generous offers."

He and Blaine rode back to the ranch late in the afternoon, neither of them pleased with the outcome of the trip.

"Did they tell you why they're hesitating?" Caleb walked to a table and grabbed glasses, pouring each of them a shot of whiskey.

Blaine took the glass, leaning back in the chair. "It's interesting. The two holdouts said they weren't complaining of the price."

"They're the same two who were the most eager to sell when I first wrote to them. One is the landowner with the largest spread and a big house. The other owns the property running along the Boundary River that connects with Circle M."

"Aye. The three who agreed have the smallest spreads. It's the two others who make the deal worthwhile."

"Did any of them mention being visited by men wanting to buy the properties?"

Blaine sat up, glancing at Bay. "Nae, Caleb. They said nothing to us about other buyers. Why?"

"Three men rode onto the ranch yesterday as Heather and Geneen were mucking the barn." Caleb continued, telling them what he knew and what the women told them. He finished by relaying the veiled threats. "I'm thinking these same men visited your sellers, intimidating them into reconsidering their decision to sell to the MacLarens."

Bay threaded fingers through his hair. "It's what I feared. Someone found out about the deals and alerted financiers in San Francisco. Did the men mention any names?"

Caleb shook his head. "No. I'm certain they'll be back."

"It may be worth going back, asking the two if they've received offers from anyone else."

"Aye. It's a good thought, Bay. We can ride out again tomorrow morning." Blaine finished his whiskey, setting the glass down. "It would be good knowing who the other buyers are."

"I'd wager the gunmen they hired don't know the names of those investing. It's common for several men to partner, hiding their identities behind a business name. I'll send August a telegram, asking him to do some checking. Of course, that will take time."

"And we may not be having much time."

Bay nodded, glancing at the wall clock. "If I leave now, I'll reach the telegraph office before it closes."

"I'll be going with you. I want to send a telegram to Ewan." Blaine didn't add he intended to send one to Lia, too. He didn't question the notion of letting her know he'd left town.

"Then we'd best get started."

Nate finished the last order for Marcus, then stood to loosen his back, stretching his arms above his head. His thoughts turned to Geneen, wondering if she'd returned from rounding up and moving the cattle, now busying herself with preparing supper. He looked forward to scrubbing away the dirt and returning to the ranch.

First, he'd meet Colt at the Lucky Lady. He'd returned the wagon to Marcus earlier in the day, asking Nate to join him. In truth, he'd rather ride straight to the ranch and see Geneen.

Striding along the boardwalk, he stopped more than once to accept congratulations from grateful townsfolk. Nate tried to push aside the praise, citing the others who'd been there, but they wouldn't have it.

He hadn't realized the extent of their dislike for Sheriff Polk until he heard stories of the way the man treated the people, his disdain for their common way of life. More than one person referred to him as a bully. When he asked why they hadn't run him out of town, he discovered they were afraid he'd come back and kill them. The cycle of intimidation and fear made Nate's blood run cold.

Disengaging himself from a group of older women, he continued to the Lucky Lady, seeing a wagon loaded with people and supplies come up the street. Halting, his breath caught in his lungs. He reached out, supporting himself against a post as they continued past.

Chinese laborers, no doubt headed for the Acorn Gold Mine. Nate felt beads of sweat form on his forehead, his breathing coming in ragged gasps.

"Are you all right, Nate?"

Blinking to clear his head, he sucked in a deep breath, noticing Colt beside him. Nodding, he turned to face him. "I'm fine. You still up for that drink?"

Colt studied him, wondering what bothered his friend. "I am. Let's get inside and find us a table."

While Colt spoke of his trip to Conviction, Nate thought of what he'd seen. He thought Settlers Valley safe from what he considered the source of opium, chastising himself for believing any town could avoid the drug for long.

"Brodie made the decision not to charge Miranda Harris with any crimes. With Black dead, there's no one who can counter her story. If she's guilty of a crime, she'll take it to the grave."

Nate rolled the whiskey glass between his fingers. "I'm sure Brodie will keep watch on her activities. He's not one to take partial measures if he believes there's any threat to the town."

Colt pushed his hat back, taking a sip of his drink. "Do you want to tell me what happened outside?"

Nate shook his head. "It wasn't much. A group of Chinese workers passing through town on their way to the mine."

Slow understanding crossed Colt's face. "You're past that, you know."

Nate startled. "What do you mean?"

"You've conquered your need for opium. From what I see, you're the same man I worked with in Nacogdoches. If those Chinese have the drug with them, which I'm almost certain they do, it won't matter this time."

"What of others who might get lured into using it?"

Staring down into his remaining whiskey, Colt shook his head. "You can't save people from themselves, Nate."

Before he could respond, the door of the saloon opened, Blaine and Bay stepping inside. Holding up his hand, Nate motioned them over, then signaled the barmaid for more glasses.

"You just get back?"

Blaine took off his hat, tossing it onto a chair. "This afternoon."

"How'd it go?"

Blaine sipped his drink, explaining what happened. "I guess you already know about the three men who threatened the lasses."

Nate pushed aside the anger at anyone intimidating Geneen. "We talked of it at supper last night. I've already spoken to Marcus, and I'm going to be spending more time at the ranch until all this is settled."

A loud commotion near the front drew their attention. Three men took over a table, shoving the lone occupant aside. Taking his chair, they laughed as he hit the floor, scrambling away.

Nate started to rise, stopping when Colt grabbed his arm. "Hold on. Let's see what they do."

The four watched as the three newcomers tossed back one whiskey after another, their voices rising as the alcohol took control. The laughter became more belligerent, taunting others at nearby tables. Several customers finished their drinks or cards and left, shaking their heads as they walked outside. When one of the three grabbed a waitress and hauled her onto his lap, refusing her protests to let her go, Blaine jumped to his feet.

"Here we go," Nate mumbled, standing to follow.

"I'm believing the lady wants you to let her go, lad." Blaine planted his feet close to the man holding the woman, his arms loose at his sides. "It'd be best to do as she asks."

The young man tightened his hold on her, glaring up. "What I do is none of your business. Now, get out of here." He relaxed his grip enough to move his hand toward his gun.

"That would be a very bad move, lad." Blaine noticed Nate beside him, guessing Bay and Colt were close by.

"He's right." Nate stepped closer. "Let the woman go and get back to your drinks. No one wants any trouble."

Shoving the woman off his lap and onto the floor, the man stood, as did his two companions. "This is none of your business. I'm telling you for the last time. Get out of here." His hand moved toward his revolver, only to feel the sting of a bullet hitting the handle of his gun.

Bay stood several feet away, his gun still aimed at the man. "It'd be best to do as we say. Finish your drinks and leave. No one wants your kind of business in here."

The three strangers looked around, seeing the guns of the four men pointed at them. The bartender held a shotgun, while several others in the saloon had drawn their six-shooters.

Surrounded, the leader of the three glared at Blaine. "This isn't the end. We've as much right to be in here as anyone."

Moving forward, Nate held the man's irate stare. "We don't take kindly to bullies. You want to come in for drinks and cards, you're welcome. Otherwise, head out. Find a place more hospitable to your kind."

Lifting an arm, the leader of the three pointed a finger at Blaine. "You've bought yourself a lot of trouble, mister." Grabbing his glass, he threw back the last of his whiskey, slamming it on the table. "Come on, boys. Let's get out of here."

Patrons in the saloon waited as the three left, not lowering their weapons until they mounted and rode off.

Nate turned to the bartender. "Do you know those men?"

"Never seen them before. Thanks for what you did. I don't want their kind in here."

Shifting toward the table where the men had been, something prickled at the edge of Nate's mind. Three men new to town. All looking to be no more than nineteen or twenty. Cocky and arrogant. Slamming his hand on the table, he mumbled a string of curses.

"What is it, lad?"

He looked at Blaine, nostrils flaring. "I may be wrong, but those are the three who threatened the women and intimidated the ranchers." Hissing out another curse, he scrubbed a hand down his face. "I let them get away."

Blaine's long strides carried him to the front. Stepping outside, he looked up and down the street, a wicked grin crossing his face. He walked back inside to where Nate stood at the bar, along with Bay and Colt.

Blaine clasped him on the shoulder. "Nae, lad. You didn't lose them. Their horses are down the street in front of Mrs. Keach's boardinghouse."

"Dahlia's..." Colt's voice trailed off as he thought of the widow and her small establishment. "She has three rooms. I have one, a young photographer another. The salesman vacated his room two days ago. They must've rented it."

Bay leaned against the bar. "Good. We know where they're staying. What do we do now?"

A mischievous grin turned up the corners of Nate's mouth. "We keep them there."

"You're certain that will do it, Mrs. Keach?"

Dahlia stopped stirring the noon meal, shooting Colt an indulgent smile. "Young man, do you doubt my ability?"

He glanced behind him at the table where Nate, Bay, and Blaine watched, chuckling at her response.

"No, ma'am. What I mean is, this isn't your everyday fare...is it?" His brows furrowed, thinking of all the meals he'd eaten in her dining room.

Patting his arm, she went back to stirring. "Don't worry, Mr. Dye. I've never served this recipe to my guests." Her eyes gleamed when she looked up. "Until now."

"What you're making won't kill them, will it?" Nate still wasn't sure he backed the plan, but no one else offered a more expedient solution.

"Of course not, Mr. Hollis. This will keep them in bed for a few days, then make them think twice about eating for several days following." Setting down the spoon, she crossed her arms. "To think those men are such bullies, threatening Mrs. Stewart and Miss MacGregor the way they did. I knew they were trouble the moment they walked in. If I'd known, I never would've rented to them." Moving to a cupboard, she pulled something down, adding it to the concoction on the stove. "Why, those three lazy men upstairs haven't stirred all morning. Missed breakfast altogether. I'll make certain they won't miss dinner, though." She stirred with a new enthusiasm.

Drinking the last of his coffee, Nate set the cup down, pulling out his pocket watch. "It's almost noon, gentlemen. It might be best for us to wait outside...in case Mrs. Keach needs our help."

Dahlia turned an indignant glare on him. "Although I appreciate the thought, I won't be needing your help, Mr. Hollis. Now, scoot along. We don't want any witnesses, do we?" A slight lilt to her voice told them how much she enjoyed being involved in their plan.

Colt crossed the short distance to the kitchen door in three strides. "I can't thank you enough, Mrs. Keach."

"Thanks isn't necessary, Mr. Dye. I can't recall the last time I had this much fun."

Hiding their grins, the four men left the woman to her potion, congregating outside on the boardwalk.

"I know you three are anxious to return to the ranch. I'll stay here. No matter what Mrs. Keach says, I'm not leaving her alone with those three."

Blaine held out his hand, grasping Colt's. "It's a brilliant idea, lad. Heather and Geneen won't stop laughing when they hear of it."

Nate and Bay also shook his hand before turning toward the livery to retrieve their horses.

"You'll send word about how those boys are doing?" Nate asked.

Colt made a slight bow. "It will be my pleasure to ride out to the ranch myself."

Blaine nodded. "Good. Then you'll be staying for supper tonight, lad. Bay and I ride out early tomorrow to talk to the last two ranchers. This time, I expect we'll return with different answers."

"Within a few minutes, those boys were holding their stomachs, running upstairs to their room. I've never seen anything like it." Colt shook his head, chuckling at the effect Dahlia's meal had on the three boarders. "I'd describe the noises coming from their room, but I'm afraid it would be too indelicate in mixed company."

Geneen swiped tears of laughter from her face. "After all you know of us, Colt, you think Heather and I are too weak to hear the rest?"

Holding up his hands, he grinned. "Never. I'd never want to face the two of you alone." Finishing the story, no one at the table had a dry eye. The idea couldn't have been simpler or more effective.

"I'm still surprised Mrs. Keach went along with it." Nate held his cup of coffee in front of him, his eyes gleaming.

"When you get to know Dahlia as well as I do, you'll understand she lives for this type of deception." Leaning back in his chair, Colt crossed his arms. "Don't misunderstand. The woman has a huge heart and is loyal. She also has no patience for people who don't show respect or try to pull something over on her. Once she heard how they'd treated Heather and Geneen, and the people in the Lucky Lady, she insisted on helping." He shook his head. "All I asked for was something to mess with their stomachs for a few hours. How was I to know the widow has a vast knowledge of poisons and ways of poisoning food? The woman is beyond description."

"I, for one, am happy with the solution." Caleb leaned forward in his chair. "It's not easy worrying about what's happening here while I'm out with the cattle."

Bay rubbed his jaw. "My guess is once those men finally feel well enough to ride on, they'll be heading back to San Francisco."

Blaine slapped his hands on the table. "Let's hope so, lad. I'm heading up to bed. Bay and I plan to leave at dawn tomorrow. When we return, I'll be reporting the MacLarens are now the owners of thousands more acres, and our families will once more be working side by side."

Chapter Twenty-Two

The rain hadn't let up all morning. It started minutes before Blaine and Bay rode north, pelting them with bullet-sized drops. Undeterred, they donned slickers, adjusting their hats low on their foreheads.

Caleb, Heather, and Geneen waited inside, hoping the fierce storm would blow past without causing too much delay in their work. Nate waited with them. He'd already told Marcus he wouldn't be working today.

"Coffee?" Geneen held the pot toward him.

"I've had three cups already, but thanks." He patted the open space on the sofa. "Sit down."

"All right, but you can't start anything. Heather and Caleb are working in his office." She nodded toward the closed door, then sat next to him.

"I wouldn't think of it." Draping an arm across her shoulders, he leaned over, kissing the corner of her mouth. He kept up his gentle persuasion until she turned to him, accepting the kiss. The sound of Caleb clearing his throat had her jumping away.

He did his best to hide a grin. "I'm going out to the barn."

"I'll go with you." Giving Geneen one more kiss, Nate stood, sliding into a slicker Caleb handed him, then went out the door.

"From what I'm seeing, you and Nate are doing grand." Heather sat next to her, letting out a tired breath.

"We seem to be doing very well. I don't know what it all means, except I want to be with him no matter what problems he faces. It may sound ridiculous, but he needs me, Heather."

"It's not ridiculous, lass. It seems Nate finally agrees with you. He'd be an eejit to do anything to jeopardize another chance." She rested her hands on her stomach, leaning back. "If Caleb hadn't given me another chance, I'd still be at Circle M and he'd be here."

"And you'd both be miserable."

Closing her eyes, Heather nodded. "Aye, we would."

"You tired? Why don't you take a nap while I start dinner?"

"Nae. I'd feel awful if Caleb walked in and saw me sleeping."

"Nonsense. He'd rather have you getting rest than pushing yourself." Standing, Geneen held out her hand. "Come on. I'll help you up."

"I'm not a lazy oaf, Geneen."

Laughing, she continued to hold out her hand. "Of course you aren't. Now, take my hand."

When they were both standing, Geneen stilled. "Wait. What do you hear?"

"Nothing."

Dashing to the window, they looked out to see clear skies, the wet dirt beginning to dry.

"I didn't hear it stop. I'll go see if the men need any help." Geneen got a couple steps before she stopped. "First, I should see to dinner."

"Nae, you go. I'll warm the food. Tell the lads to come in when they're ready."

"That's it, Geneen. Keep going." Nate encouraged her from where he and Caleb stood outside the corral. "You almost have him."

Geneen stayed focused, doing everything she remembered from the lessons Blaine and Fletcher gave her at Circle M. With all their words of praise, they'd never let her break a horse on her own.

"That's it, lass. You're doing grand." Heather waved her hand in the air from her spot a few feet from Caleb.

"She's going to do it, Heather." Caleb kissed her, then turned his attention back to Geneen.

Nate jumped on the lowest rail of the corral, resting his arms on top. "A little more and he's yours, sweetheart." A huge smile broke across his face when the gelding began to settle. "A little more. Just a little more."

Caleb let out a loud whoop when the gelding snorted, danced a few more times, snorted again, then gave in to the inevitable.

"You've done it, Geneen. Now, walk him around the corral, let him get used to your weight." Nate turned to Caleb. "She did it."

"I always knew she could. Ewan wouldn't allow Blaine and Fletcher to let her on a horse they hadn't already calmed." Caleb wrapped an arm around Heather, both watching Geneen guide the horse in a large circle.

After a few minutes, Nate opened the gate, moving with measured, slow steps toward Geneen. He whispered to the horse, reaching out to stroke the animal's neck when Geneen stopped.

"You did great. Go ahead and get down. I'll take him to the barn and cool him down." Taking the reins, Nate watched her slide to the ground, his eyes showing the pride he felt.

"I'll come with you." She walked next to him, stopping at the sound of approaching horses. "It's Blaine and Bay. They weren't gone long."

"There were just the two ranches to visit. With luck, their meetings went well. You go meet them. I'll take care of the horse."

She ran through the open gate, closing it behind her. Caleb and Heather were already by their side, throwing questions at them.

"Bay did a fine job explaining about the three lads and their lies." Blaine slapped Bay on the back.

"Did they agree to the original terms?" Caleb asked.

Bay nodded. "They did. Once we told them the three men would no longer be a problem, they signed the initial agreement. Now I have to draw up final contracts and it will all be settled."

"Which means we'll be making a visit to the lads before they leave town." Blaine looked at Bay and Caleb. "They need to be understanding they've no more hand to play. They'll be returning to their bosses defeated, and no longer welcome in Settlers Valley."

Caleb turned to look at Heather. "We need to ride into town right away and deliver the message."

"Before they're over the effects of Dahlia's meal," Bay added.

Blaine nodded. "Aye. They'll be more receptive in their current condition."

Heather squeezed Caleb's arm. "Well, get on with you then. By the time you return, Geneen and I will have supper waiting."

Settlers Valley

"Hey," the leader of the three groaned, feeling himself being lifted by the collar. "Let me be." His voice hissed out, his hands clutching his stomach. "You've no business with us."

"Ach, that's not true, laddie. We're the most important people you'll be seeing in this part of the country. What's your name?"

Sending Blaine a blurry-eyed stare, he shook his head. "My name's not your business. What do you want?"

Bay and Caleb held the other two in a similar way, their captives moaning, bending at the waist. Nate rested his shoulder against the doorframe, watching.

Blaine shook the one in his grip. "You've been threatening ranchers with nonsense about their land. You'll no longer be welcome on their properties. They've signed contracts—*binding* contracts, which no court in the land will contradict." The man looked up at him, his eyes glassy and remote. "When you can ride, you'll be saddling your horses and leaving town, never to return to Settlers Valley. If we see you here again, you'll be needing more than horses to leave a second time." Dropping him back to the mattress, Blaine leaned down. "Are we in agreement?"

The man nodded, then rolled to his side, his body shaking. Bay and Caleb dropped their men in the same fashion, turning to leave.

"Ach, I almost forgot." Blaine grabbed a handful of money from the dresser, counting it out. "I'll be paying Mrs. Keach in advance." He shook the coins in his hand. "You'll not be taking advantage of such a lovely woman."

Blaine followed the others into the hall, halting when the leader called out.

"Who are you?"

He turned. "Blaine. Blaine MacLaren."

"You'll send someone to fetch me if they give you any problems, right?" Nate stood before Dahlia, seeing the hard set of her jaw.

"Young man, I'll have you know I can take care of myself. Besides, Mr. Dye has been keeping watch on those three ruffians. Twice he's had to convince them to stay in their room."

"Where is he now?"

"He's at some meeting with Marcus Kamm and a few other businessmen at the church. You might want to stop by there before you leave

303

town, Mr. Hollis. They may want a word with you."

Nate could hear chuckles behind him, knowing Caleb, Blaine, and Bay had heard the suggestion.

"Thank you, Mrs. Keach. I just might do that."

Walking to their horses, the others refused to ride to the ranch. They followed behind Nate as he made the short ride to the church. Not content to wait outside, they followed him in, removing their hats as they entered.

At the sound of boots stomping down the aisle, Marcus and the others turned. "Ah, there's Nate now. Come on up and join us. You, too, fellas." He waved his arm, motioning for them all to take seats.

"What's this about, Marcus?" Nate noted the others in attendance, including Colt.

"Well now, we've been discussing how we need a new sheriff and who we might select. Seems there's just one man in Settlers Valley who meets all the qualifications. Colt has been filling us in on your work in Texas and Conviction. It's pretty impressive."

The reverend stepped forward. "What Marcus is trying to say is we'd like you to be our sheriff, Nate. You'd get a decent wage, a room and meals at Mrs. Keach's place, and free board for your horse at Marcus's livery."

"And free whiskey at the Lucky Lady." Nate looked down a pew at the bartender. "I tend the bar...and own the place."

Marcus stood, locking his gaze on him. "What do you say, Nate? Everyone in town feels the same about you taking the job."

"What about my work for you?"

Marcus shrugged. "We don't have a lot of troublemakers in town. I figure you can help me out when things are slow."

Nate glanced at Colt, who nodded, then behind him at his friends. The smiles on their faces told him all he needed to know. Taking a breath, he blew it out.

"Well, gentlemen, I'd be honored to be your sheriff. When do you want me to start?"

Highlander Ranch

"Why didn't *you* take the job, Colt? You're more qualified than me." Nate looked across the supper table, his hand resting on Geneen's knee.

An easy grin appeared on his face. "I already told you. As lovely as Settlers Valley is, I need a little more going on. Besides, I've already got a job."

"You'll be riding back to Texas?" Caleb forked another mouthful of beef.

"I'm taking a little time off. I thought I'd ride to Conviction, maybe head over to San Francisco for a spell. See some of the sights before returning to Texas."

"I'm leaving the day after tomorrow. You can ride with me."

Colt nodded at Bay. "I believe I'll do that."

Geneen felt a wave of sadness. Colt and Bay would be leaving. Nate's job meant he'd be living at the boardinghouse. Being the only lawman, he wouldn't be able to spend many weekends at the ranch. She had the sick feeling of losing him all over again.

Conversations continued with glasses raised to Circle M expanding and Nate's new job. She and Heather served dessert and coffee, but Geneen couldn't feel the enthusiasm she knew she should. She loved Nate with all her heart. The new job might make all her dreams fall away as they had when he'd ridden away all those months ago.

"If no one minds, I'd like to go for a walk with Geneen." He didn't wait for them to respond before grabbing her hand and helping her up. "It's cold out tonight. We'd better get our coats."

Slipping into hers, she remained silent. Their other walks had been fun, memories she etched in her mind. It frightened her to think tonight's would be different.

He intertwined their fingers as they walked down the porch steps. "Do you mind going back to the river?"

"No. I love it there."

They didn't speak as they made their way along the trail to the fallen log. The moon wasn't as full and clouds hung low in the sky, making it harder for their eyes to adjust. She followed his lead, stopping when he pointed out the log.

Sitting down, he didn't let go of her hand, holding it in his lap as he stared out over the water.

Geneen shifted on the log, clearing her throat. "I haven't had a chance to congratulate you on the new job. You'll make a wonderful sheriff, Nate." She squeezed his hand, hoping he didn't hear the tremble in her voice.

"Thank you. I wasn't certain I'd take it until the reverend offered it to me. The moment he said the words, I knew it was what I wanted."

Biting her lower lip, she nodded. Pushing aside her hesitancy, she looked up into his face. "I suppose you'll be staying in town most of the time. I mean, being the only lawman, it will be hard to come to the ranch at nights and on weekends."

His features softened. "Nope. When the others left the church, I stayed behind for a few minutes to talk with Marcus and the reverend. I told them I'd be living at the ranch, only using the room at Mrs. Keach's when I had to. I let them know my future wife worked on the ranch and I had no intention of spending my nights away from her."

Geneen's breath caught, a startled gasp escaping her lips. Blinking to stall the sudden moisture in her eyes, she held his gaze. "Your future wife?"

"I figured you wouldn't want to live in town, and I'm definitely not sleeping alone. What do you say, Geneen. I love you. Are you willing to give a battered ex-soldier a chance by marrying him?"

Placing a hand over her mouth, she did her best to stop a sob from escaping.

"Are you all right, sweetheart?"

Nodding, she took a deep breath, settling the fluttering in her stomach.

"Marry me, Geneen. You won't regret it."

Bursting into a combination of tears and laughter, she nodded. "I love you so much, Nate. Yes. I'll marry you."

Epilogue

Three weeks later...
Circle M Ranch

A large group of MacLarens stood together, enjoying the clear, chilly day. Nate kept his arm around Geneen, unwilling to let his new bride even be a few feet away. He still couldn't quite believe she'd agreed to marry him. The one woman who had enough faith to stand by him and not give up when others would've walked away.

Once Geneen's letter reached the aunts, telling of their betrothal, plans were quickly arranged for their wedding to coincide with Heather's trip to see Doctor Tilden. The haste hadn't bothered Nate. He wanted her as his wife as soon as possible, and having the wedding at Circle M pleased everyone. It also gave them a chance to see Sean once more before he left for Edinburgh.

"Are you certain you're ready, lad? Scotland is a long way from the ranch." Fletcher settled an arm over Sean's shoulders.

Although a few inches shorter than most men in the family, quiet, with a lean build, no one could mistake Sean's features as anything other than a MacLaren. He smiled, affably shrugging off his cousin's arm.

"Aye. It's what I've wanted for years."

His younger sister, Bridget, threaded her arm through his. "You know we'll be missing you."

Sean kissed her cheek. "And I'll be missing you, lassie." Looking up, he glanced around the large circle of family. They were his entire world, and he was about to leave them behind for a future he still couldn't define. "I'll be missing all of you." His soft voice fractured a little.

"I'm still not understanding why you need to cross an ocean for education when you're already the finest veterinarian for hundreds of miles." His mother, Gail, leaned against her husband's side.

"Now, Gail. You'll not be making the lad feel bad about leaving. He wants the formal education, and no matter the distance, he's going to fulfill his dream." Ian's features remained passive, the moisture in his eyes revealing his inner feelings. "We're all proud of you, laddie."

Holding up his glass, Sean cleared his throat. "This isn't a day for sorrow. It's a day for celebrating the marriage of Nate and Geneen, and the coming wee bairn."

Lifting their glasses, they acknowledged Sean's sentiments. Glancing around the group, Colin cocked his head at his brother, Camden.

"Where's Blaine?"

Nate looked at Geneen. He knew she and Blaine had a brief conversation after the ceremony. Not long after, he'd ridden toward town.

"He had some business in Conviction." Geneen took a sip of punch, mindful of the surprised expressions.

"The lad rode off on your wedding day?" Colin asked, his voice holding a bit of censure.

Geneen nodded. "He asked if I minded, and I told him no."

Colin shook his head, a little miffed about his brother's actions. "What in the world could be more important than being with family?"

Brodie and Fletcher shared a look, faint smiles tipping up the corners of their mouths.

Conviction

Blaine sat alone at a table in the Gold Dust, his gaze locked on the young woman moving about the room. Saturday afternoons brought a varied group of people into the restaurant— couples, cowhands, businessmen passing through. All looking for a quiet, decent meal before continuing their day.

All Blaine desired was time with Lia. Not a lot. Just enough to tell her goodbye.

311

"More coffee, Mr. MacLaren?" She held the pot above his cup, a brow quirked.

"I've told you my name is Blaine, lass." He held up his cup, staring into her amazing turquoise eyes with golden brown highlights.

She glanced around the restaurant, then nodded. "Blaine."

His name rolled off her lips in a soft whoosh, causing his body to tighten.

"I've not seen you in the restaurant in a while."

Shaking his head, Blaine set the cup down. "I've been gone on business."

"Ah, that would explain it. Welcome home." She turned to leave, stopping when he gripped her arm.

"I came in to tell you I'm leaving Conviction."

Her body stilled, a bleak expression replacing the joy he'd seen a moment before. "Leaving?"

"Aye. The family purchased more ranches north of here. I'm being sent to run the properties."

"I see." Lifting her chin, Lia did her best to hide the disappointment in his leaving. "Your family must think highly of you."

Right now, what his family thought meant little to him. What captured his interest stood a foot away, a despondent look in her eyes.

"The ranch is a short ride east of Settlers Valley."

She knew the name, understood the town to be several hours north, possibly too far for him to visit. The thought brought a dull ache to her chest.

"I've heard of it. From what I know, it's quite a ride."

He nodded. "About five hours."

She offered a hollow grin. "Too far to stop in for a meal and coffee."

Until this moment, Blaine hadn't realized how much he wanted to see her again. "I'll be back when I can."

"I've heard such words before and know it's an empty thought." Sucking in a breath, she forced a smile. "It's been a pleasure to know you." She turned, taking a few steps away.

"Lia, wait."

Stopping, she cast him a wistful expression. "Goodbye, Mr. Blaine MacLaren."

Thank you for taking the time to read Nate's Destiny. If you enjoyed it, please consider telling your friends or posting a short review. Word of mouth is an author's best friend and much appreciated.

Watch for book seven in the MacLarens of Boundary Mountain series, Blaine's Wager.

Please join my reader's group to be notified of my New Releases at:
https://www.shirleendavies.com/contact-me.html

I care about quality, so if you find something in error, please contact me via email at
shirleen@shirleendavies.com

About the Author

Shirleen Davies writes romance—historical and contemporary western romance with a touch of suspense. She is the best-selling author of the MacLarens of Fire Mountain Series, the MacLarens of Boundary Mountain Series, and the Redemption Mountain Series. Shirleen grew up in Southern California, attended Oregon State University, and has degrees from San Diego State University and the University of Maryland. Her passion is writing emotionally charged stories of flawed people who find redemption through love and acceptance. She lives with her husband in a beautiful town in northern Arizona. Between them, they have five adult sons who are their greatest achievements.

I love to hear from my readers!

Send me an email: shirleen@shirleendavies.com
Visit my Website: www.shirleendavies.com
Sign up to be notified of New Releases:
www.shirleendavies.com
Check out all of my Books:
www.shirleendavies.com/books.html
Comment on my Blog:
www.shirleendavies.com/blog.html
Follow me on Amazon:
http://www.amazon.com/author/shirleendavies

Follow my on BookBub:
https://www.bookbub.com/authors/shirleen-davies

Other ways to connect with me:

Facebook Author Page:
http://www.facebook.com/shirleendaviesauthor
Twitter: www.twitter.com/shirleendavies
Pinterest: http://pinterest.com/shirleendavies
Instagram:
https://www.instagram.com/shirleendavies_author/
Google Plus:
https://plus.google.com/+ShirleenDaviesAuthor

Books by Shirleen Davies
Historical Western Romance Series
MacLarens of Fire Mountain

Tougher than the Rest, Book One
Faster than the Rest, Book Two
Harder than the Rest, Book Three
Stronger than the Rest, Book Four
Deadlier than the Rest, Book Five
Wilder than the Rest, Book Six

Redemption Mountain

Redemption's Edge, Book One
Wildfire Creek, Book Two
Sunrise Ridge, Book Three
Dixie Moon, Book Four
Survivor Pass, Book Five
Promise Trail, Book Six
Deep River, Book Seven
Courage Canyon, Book Eight
Forsaken Falls, Book Nine
Solitude Gorge, Book Ten, Coming next in the
series!

MacLarens of Boundary Mountain

Colin's Quest, Book One,
Brodie's Gamble, Book Two

Quinn's Honor, Book Three
Sam's Legacy, Book Four
Heather's Choice, Book Five
Nate's Destiny, Book Six
Blaine's Wager, Book Seven, Coming next in the series!

<u>Contemporary Romance Series</u>

MacLarens of Fire Mountain

Second Summer, Book One
Hard Landing, Book Two
One More Day, Book Three
All Your Nights, Book Four
Always Love You, Book Five
Hearts Don't Lie, Book Six
No Getting Over You, Book Seven
'Til the Sun Comes Up, Book Eight
Foolish Heart, Book Nine
Forever Love, Book Ten, Coming next in the series!

Peregrine Bay

Reclaiming Love, Book One, A Novella
Our Kind of Love, Book Two

Burnt River

Shane's Burden, Book One by Peggy Henderson
Thorn's Journey, Book Two by Shirleen Davies
Aqua's Achilles, Book Three by Kate Cambridge
Ashley's Hope, Book Four by Amelia Adams
Harpur's Secret, Book Five by Kay P. Dawson
Mason's Rescue, Book Six by Peggy L. Henderson
Del's Choice, Book Seven by Shirleen Davies
Ivy's Search, Book Eight by Kate Cambridge
Phoebe's Fate, Book Nine by Amelia Adams
Brody's Shelter, Book Ten by Kay P. Dawson
Boone's Surrender, Book Eleven by Shirleen Davies
Watch for more books in the series!

Find all of my books at:
https://www.shirleendavies.com/books.html

Avalanche Ranch Press, LLC
PO Box 12618
Prescott, AZ 86304

Nate's Destiny is a work of fiction. Names,
characters, places, and incidents are either
products of the author's imagination or used
fictitiously. Any resemblance to actual events,
locales, or persons, living or dead, is wholly
coincidental.